His goal had been ~~with her.~~

It had not been to like it.

Falling for Jacinth would undermine the most important investigation of his life. Yet, he was falling, and falling hard.

It wasn't just the physical attraction, though that was dynamite. It was everything about her.

He felt this fierce need to protect her, but the one she needed protection from most was him. He couldn't keep his hands off her. And that kiss last night had equaled the thrill of having sex with any other woman he'd ever been with. Pulling away and leaving her at the door had been downright painful.

None of that changed what he had to do, but he couldn't be lover and destroyer. He'd have to put the skids on any romantic involvement.

His mind understood that. His body was the traitor.

JOANNA WAYNE

STRANGER, SEDUCER, PROTECTOR

TORONTO NEW YORK LONDON
AMSTERDAM PARIS SYDNEY HAMBURG
STOCKHOLM ATHENS TOKYO MILAN MADRID
PRAGUE WARSAW BUDAPEST AUCKLAND

TO ALL MY READERS WHO LOVE NEW ORLEANS AND THE MYSTERY AND ROMANCE IT INSPIRES. AND A SPECIAL SMILE AND WAVE TO ALL LOUISIANA FRIENDS AND FAMILY.

Recycling programs
for this product may
not exist in your area.

ISBN-13: 978-0-373-69575-1

STRANGER, SEDUCER, PROTECTOR

ABOUT THE AUTHOR

Joanna Wayne was born and raised in Shreveport, Louisiana, and received her undergraduate and graduate degrees from LSU-Shreveport. She moved to New Orleans in 1984, and it was there that she attended her first writing class and joined her first professional writing organization. Her debut novel, *Deep in the Bayou,* was published in 1994.

Now, dozens of published books later, Joanna has made a name for herself as being on the cutting edge of romantic suspense in both series and single-title novels. She has been on the Waldenbooks bestseller list for romance and has won many industry awards. She is also a popular speaker at writing organizations and local community functions and has taught creative writing at the University of New Orleans Metropolitan College.

Joanna currently resides in a small community forty miles north of Houston, Texas, with her husband. Though she still has many family and emotional ties to Louisiana, she loves living in the Lone Star State. You may write Joanna at P.O. Box 852, Montgomery, Texas 77356.

Books by Joanna Wayne

HARLEQUIN INTRIGUE
  955—MAVERICK CHRISTMAS
  975—24/7
1001—24 KARAT AMMUNITION*
1019—TEXAS GUN SMOKE*
1041—POINT BLANK PROTECTOR*
1065—LOADED*
1096—MIRACLE AT COLTS RUN CROSS*
1123—COWBOY COMMANDO†
1152—COWBOY TO THE CORE†
1167—BRAVO, TANGO, COWBOY†
1195—COWBOY DELIRIUM*†
1228—COWBOY SWAGGER**
1249—GENUINE COWBOY**
1264—AK-COWBOY**
1289—COWBOY FEVER**
1308—STRANGER, SEDUCER, PROTECTOR

*Four Brothers of Colts Run Cross
†Special Ops Texas
**Sons of Troy Ledger

CAST OF CHARACTERS

Nick Bruno—He's dead set on only one thing—until he meets Jacinth Villaré.

Jacinth Villaré—The sprawling Esplanade Avenue mansion she and her sister have inherited has turned into a nightmare.

Elton Bruno—Nick's father. He's spent most of his adult life in prison for a crime he claims he didn't commit.

Caitlyn Villaré—Jacinth's sister, who is away on her honeymoon.

Dr. Reginald Jefferies—Jacinth's professor friend and mentor.

Detective Ron Greene—He's determined to make an arrest.

Joy Adams, Cecelia Davis and Jewel Benet—Three New Orleans exotic dancers who disappeared without a trace.

Sophie and Micah Villaré—Jacinth's parents, no longer living.

Marie Villaré—Jacinth's grandmother, who willed her and Caitlyn the aging mansion.

Luther Villaré—Micah Villaré's half brother.

Carrie Marks—Luther's girlfriend before he was murdered.

Gladys Findley—Jacinth's next-door neighbor.

Eric Ledeaux—An old friend of Marie's before her death, and a spurned lover of Joy Adams's.

Billy Raquet—Carrie Marks's current boyfriend.

Bill and Eugenia Kibecti—Friends of Dr. Jefferies who own a historic home with a secret passageway.

Sarah Livingston—Joy Adams's roommate when Joy disappeared.

Chapter One

Her heart pounded and cold sweat trickled down her face and between her breasts. There was no mistaking the creaks of the aged floorboards outside her room.

He was there, pacing, watching, anticipating the moment when he would place his cold, meaty fingers around her neck and squeeze the breath from her lungs.

The doorbell rang. Jacinth Villaré's heart jumped to her throat and the gritty suspense novel she'd been reading slipped from her hands and slapped against the blue quilt. Apprehension lingered. Who would be visiting this time of night?

She glanced at the clock next to her bed. It was only ten after ten, not really considered late in the Big Easy, though Jacinth had snuggled into bed with her book a full hour ago.

The visitor at the door was likely a lost tourist looking for the bed-and-breakfast where he'd rented a room for the night. There were two in Jacinth's block alone, one owned by the friendly gay couple who lived just to the right of her.

The bell rang again. She untangled herself from the

crisp percale sheets, threw her legs over the side of the bed and felt the familiar tingle of old wool as her heels and toes caressed the worn rug.

She reached back for the book to tuck it beneath the covers, and then realized the act would be a waste of time.

Romantic suspense was her secret escape from the stacks of historically accurate novels and legitimate works of nonfiction that defined her serious, academic persona.

But no one would be visiting her bedroom tonight.

Unfortunately, that was also true for every other night in the recent past and likely the immediate future. Working toward her doctorate and keeping up with her duties as a teacher left no time to invest in a relationship.

Her hands automatically grabbed for her tatty chenille robe before she changed her mind and left it hanging from the bedpost. Her nightshirt covered more than the shorts and T-shirt she'd worn to rake the yard this afternoon.

She flicked the light switch at the top of the winding staircase. Shimmery illumination from the cut-glass chandelier crept over the walls like golden wings.

Repairing and cleaning the monstrous antique had taken months, but the air of opulence it provided the old family home was definitely worth the time and cost.

The floorboards creaked eerily as she traipsed the hallway of the sprawling mansion. Reaching the wide double doors, Jacinth cautiously put her eye to the peephole. The gas lantern near the front walk painted entrancing shadows across the man at her door, but did nothing to disguise his rugged masculinity.

Hard bodied, clearly evident in the black T-shirt he was wearing. Unruly dark hair peeking from beneath a Saints cap. A face with character and craggy angles. The kind of stranger you'd invite into an erotic dream— but not into your living room at ten at night.

Jacinth unlatched the door and eased it open a crack, leaving the security chain firmly in place. "Can I help you?"

"Just thought I'd warn you that you're going to have one hell of a water bill if you don't turn off your sprinkler system."

"I don't have a sprinkler system."

"Then you've got bigger problems."

She glanced past the man and at a stream of water flowing across her soggy front yard and pouring over the curb like an infinity pool.

She groaned. "Another wretched trick of this money pit posing as a house. I know the plumber better than I know my neighbors. I'll call him."

"I can locate the outside valve and turn your water off if you like. Then you could wait until morning to call him. That might save you paying double or even triple for an after-hours emergency call."

Money she didn't have to waste. "I'd appreciate that." Her wary nature checked in again. "Who are you?"

"Sorry. Guess I should have introduced myself. Name's Nick Bruno. I'm moving in next door to you."

"Into the B and B?"

"The other next door. I rented the carriage house apartment from Gladys Findley."

Bruno. The same last name as the man who'd killed her father. Not that she could hold that against this guy, unless… "You're not kin to Elton Bruno, are you?"

He looked bewildered. "Who is that?"

"Forget it."

Jacinth couldn't see the street in front of the Findley house from this angle, but she had noticed that the "furnished apartment for rent" sign had still been in place when she'd raked the latest deluge of oak leaves from the lawn late this afternoon. "When did you move in?"

"I haven't yet. I just closed the deal this afternoon and I was bringing over a few boxes tonight. I didn't expect to need rubber boots."

"Sorry. Years of neglect have left this house a catastrophe waiting to happen. I'm afraid that living next to me, you'll never know what to expect."

"Sounds intriguing."

The deep timbre of his voice coupled with a seductive smile raised her pulse more effectively than her nightly sit-ups had. "I'm Jacinth Villaré," she said, finally unlatching the safety chain and extending a hand.

Her cat appeared from nowhere and curled around Jacinth's ankle, feigning protectiveness. Jacinth reached down to pick her up, but the feline yowled and made a stealthy dart toward freedom.

"Come back here, Sin," she ordered a cat that never followed her commands.

Nick snatched up the cat before it could sink into the watery slush. "Sin? Interesting name for this bad boy."

"She's a girl. And Sin is short for Sinister, a name well deserved for her evil stare when the royal highness's dignity is affronted."

He held the cat up for Jacinth to rescue from his strong arms.

Sin arched her back and showed her claws as if ready to attack. Nick ignored her antics.

"I'd recommend filling some kitchen pots and your bathtub with water before I cut it off. But with that leak, you can expect the pressure to be low."

"Thanks. I will. Give me ten minutes."

"Perfect."

"Welcome to the neighborhood," she called as he walked away.

Jacinth hurried to the kitchen, filled a few pots for drinking water and then raced up the stairs to fill the tub in her bathroom. The pressure was indeed low, but if Hunky Nick gave her the full ten minutes, she could collect enough water to flush the commode until the leak was fixed.

Hunky Nick who was now her next-door neighbor. Probably married or gay, she cautioned a few unexpected, lustful vibes.

The bathtub was almost full when the decreased flow from the faucet turned into a trickle and then stopped altogether. Evidently, Nick had located the valve and likely saved her a fortune on her water and plumbing bills.

Married or not, the guy was handy to have around.

Now back to bed to finish the last chapter in her book, though she feared Nick's image might replace the description the author had provided for the hero. Her hand was on the doorknob when a crash behind her created a deluge of flying debris.

She spun around to find that the back wall had caved in, dropping huge chunks of plaster into her tub of previously clean water. A wall she had only last week spent hours painting.

Her spirits caved with the chalky drywall. Why had she fallen in love with a house that didn't love her back?

More plaster fell, a lump of it landing near her feet. She started to step over it. Only…

Cripes!

It wasn't plaster. It was…

A scream tore from her throat as a decaying head rolled against her bare foot and its remaining, wiry blond hair came to rest against Jacinth's toes.

Chapter Two

The scream stopped Nick in his tracks. No mistaking its origin. It had come from the second floor of the Villaré house.

Adrenaline shot through him, triggering his instincts for danger. The boxes he was carrying slipped from his grasp and crashed to the damp ground near his pickup truck. A pair of tennis shoes and some DVDs flew out of one.

He could see nothing but escaping rectangles of light from the windows of the Villaré house, but he grabbed the loaded Glock from under the driver's seat before he took off, sloshing in the mud toward the scream.

He took Jacinth's front steps two at a time, then pressed on the bell with the index finger of his left hand. His right hand held the Glock.

"Jacinth," he called. "Are you okay?"

No answer. No more screams. Nothing from the house except dead silence. The scream echoed though his mind. Hair-raising. Bloodcurdling.

He was ready to shoot off the lock when he heard footsteps approach the door.

"Who's there?"

"It's me—Nick. I heard you scream."

She unlocked the door and opened it, standing in it rather than inviting him in. Her eyes were wide, her gorgeous face a ghostly white, and her hair was covered with dust and bits of what looked like chalk.

Nick kept his finger poised near the trigger. He stretched his neck, trying to see past her and into the house. All he saw were indistinct shadows lurking in the hallway beyond the foyer.

"Is someone here with you?"

"No. At least no one who's currently alive."

"Care to explain?"

She took a deep breath and exhaled slowly as if trying to gain control. "The walls in one upstairs bathroom collapsed and a woman's head fell out of the debris and rolled across the tile." She shuddered again.

"A human head fell out of your wall?"

"I know how bizarre this must sound, but you can't say I didn't warn you about living next to me."

"Too late. I've already paid the deposit and the first month's rent."

She was trying to make light of the nightmarish situation now, but he'd heard the scream. It had vibrated with pure terror. He held the gun where she could see it.

"If there's a problem, I can help."

She hesitated, eyeing him warily, her gaze lingering on his pistol.

"Do you have a license to carry that thing?"

"A weapon, not a thing." Transferring the automatic

.45 to his left hand, he retrieved a business card from the back pocket of his jeans. He handed it to her.

She read it and then stared up at him from beneath incredibly dark and thick lashes. "So you're a private detective."

"Yep. I'm legitimate and harmless."

"That's what all the B-movie psychos say." But she finally stepped aside for him to enter.

Their bare arms brushed. The feel of satiny softness so unlike his own weathered skin caught him off guard. So did the surge of arousal that followed.

He stepped away as she closed and locked the door behind them.

He followed her up a wide, winding staircase, mesmerized by the sensuous sway of her hips. He'd never expected Jacinth Villaré to be this hot.

What he had planned might turn out to be a lot like playing catch with a hand grenade.

His sinuses rebelled as she led him into a high-ceilinged, narrow bathroom at the head of the stairs. The wall behind the tub had collapsed as if it had been shaken from its supports by a devastating earthquake. Stooping, he picked up a large chunk of plaster and turned it over in his hand a couple of times.

"This is damp. You must have a leak in the wall, as well. That's probably what caused the collapse."

"I can live with crumbling walls." She pointed at the floor next to a woven clothes hamper. "That has got to go."

He stared at the rotting head. Definitely human.

"Someone must have decapitated her and buried the

head inside the walls of the house," Jacinth said, her voice steadier and her mood seemingly calmer now that he was on the scene with her.

"Looks that way," he agreed. "I'm not sure the victim is female, though. A lot of male French Quarter inhabitants wear their hair long."

She nodded. "At least the decay explains the smell," Jacinth said.

"Not nearly as bad as I would have expected," Nick said.

"But the odor was nauseating in this room when we first took possession of the house. My sister Caitlyn was convinced it was a backup in the sewerage lines. The plumber we called assured us the smell was from something that had died in the wall. We assumed he meant something like a rat or a squirrel. It never dawned on either of us that the source of the odor might be human."

"What did you do?"

"Called an exterminator. He checked the attic, but didn't find what was causing the stench. Thankfully, he got rid of some rodents we didn't know we had. Then we hired a handyman to secure the structure to keep out future pests."

"And the sickening odor?"

"The exterminator used some kind of expensive chemical to subdue it. It took three treatments."

Nick settled on his haunches for a better look at the head. He couldn't tell how long it had been rotting in the walls, but his educated guess was no more than eighteen months.

"How long have you lived in the house?" he asked.

"Just under a year, but our first visit was immediately after my grandmother's will was probated. That was fourteen months ago."

Old murder tales went with the house like crawfish and étouffée, but it rattled Nick to think this atrocity might have taken place after Jacinth and her sister had moved in.

"Where's your sister?" he asked.

"On her honeymoon."

He hadn't realized she'd gotten married, though he'd thoroughly researched both sisters. Caitlyn was the drama queen who made a living by giving tours of the ghostly and sometimes dangerous Cities of the Dead that housed the Quarter's famed crypts and tombs. She'd nearly gotten herself killed in that capacity.

Jacinth was the quiet and studious type, a graduate student with a teaching assistantship at Tulane. Brainy and sophisticated. Unquestionably, not his type.

Too bad she was so damned attractive. And that was without a trace of makeup and with her silky, dark hair disheveled and powdered with grayish, flaky plaster.

Best not to even glance at the cotton nightshirt that skimmed her perky breasts and danced about her shapely legs.

"I'm calling the cops," Jacinth announced, "though I doubt they'll rush right over to examine a decayed body that may have been entombed in the wall for years."

Bringing in the cops at this stage of the game might complicate his mission, but there was little he could do about that now. He waited as she made the call, his mind dealing with ways to handle the new layers of intricacies.

"They're sending a uniformed officer to deal with the situation," Jacinth said once she'd broken the connection. "They said we shouldn't touch anything before he arrives—as if I would willingly touch that head. But I guess I should get Sin out of here."

Jacinth reached up to a shelf just over her head where Sin had settled, looking as if she were poised for an ambush. Jacinth's nightshirt inched up her thighs.

Nick grew instantly hard. Sin avoided Jacinth's grasping hands and pounced on Nick's back, letting her claws scrape the skin at the back of his neck before it leaped from his shoulders to the top of the clothes hamper.

Jacinth scolded the cat. The feline demonstrated the stare that had earned her name. Nick was undaunted. He figured he'd had the scratch and the stare coming to him for the thoughts he'd had about the cat's owner.

"Maybe we should go back downstairs and wait for the cop," Nick said.

"I appreciate you coming to my rescue tonight, Nick, but there's really no reason for you to stay. I'll be fine now that I've calmed down—unless the house decides to hurl the rest of the corpse at me."

"I wouldn't rule that out."

She looked back to the freakish head. "Good point. But it's late and you probably still have boxes to carry inside."

"Only a couple. And I'm a night owl. I'd be happy to stay."

"In that case, I wouldn't mind the company." Jacinth covered her mouth and coughed. "My throat feels as if I've been eating grit."

"More reason we should get out of here and close the door." In truth, he'd like nothing better than to explore behind the walls and see what other gruesome surprises might be skulking there. Only he'd prefer to do that without Jacinth looking over his shoulder or even being in the house.

Jacinth stepped over to make another stab at retrieving Sin. The cat jumped from her reach and slunk out the door.

"She's not the most cooperative of creatures," Jacinth said.

"Have you had her long?"

"She came with the house. Mrs. Findley said she'd just shown up at the back door one day, and my grandmother had taken her in. She said the cat and Marie were equally cantankerous so they got along well."

"Did your grandmother live in this house right up until she died?"

"All but the last six months of her life when she moved into a nursing/retirement center."

"Who took care of Sin during that time?"

"Mrs. Findley, and sometimes her husband. My grandmother had left cases of food and given them a key to the house. She was here before us so now Sin thinks Caitlyn and I are the strays and she's not too keen on letting us share the premises."

"Too bad she can't talk. She might be able to tell us who the head belonged to."

Jacinth ran her fingers through her hair and a new shower of dust rained down on her shoulders. "Would you excuse me while I go wash up in some of the water I saved and put on something a bit more appropriate?"

"Not at all. Take your time. If the cop shows up before you're ready, I'll let him in." And hopefully the officer would be someone new on the force who didn't know Nick. The less Jacinth learned about him the better, at least until he'd had time to win her trust.

"You can wait in the den," Jacinth called. "It's to the left of the staircase, just opposite the Louis XIV style parlor. We veered away a tad from our adherence to strict historical accuracy of design in the small den and included a comfortable couch and chair along with the antique lamps and antebellum paintings."

"I'm sure my back will appreciate that." Nick enjoyed the view as Jacinth walked away. Images of her slipping out of the nightshirt plagued his mind. A menacing yowl jerked him back to reality.

He turned to stare at Sin who was glaring at him from the bottom step. "Got it, Sin. Jacinth is off-limits for reasons even you can't fathom."

JACINTH HAD RINSED her long hair over the sink with a pan of cool water. It was still dripping when she caught sight of flashing blue lights in her driveway.

She toweled it quickly and made a mostly unsuccessful attempt to smooth it back into place. She needed a shower so badly right now that she'd have paid triple overtime for a plumber.

A quick check in the mirror assured her she looked

as ill put together as she felt. But the cream-colored sweater she'd pulled on over a pair of worn jeans was at least better than talking to a cop in her nightshirt.

She reached the top of the staircase as Nick ushered two police officers inside the door. One was tall and thin, his face ruddy and his sandy blond hair short and neatly combed. The other was probably a good ten years older than his partner. In his early forties, she'd guess, with a receding hairline and a slightly crooked nose.

She motioned for them to join her upstairs. Nick led the way, his confident swagger making him look perfectly at home in this house that still made Jacinth feel like a trespasser from time to time.

The cops flashed their badges and identified themselves. The young one was Jordon Sims. The older one was Mike Jones. His expression held a tinge of aggravation as if he expected this was some kind of teenage hoax.

She introduced herself and got what sounded more like a grunt than a greeting in return. Mike immediately turned his attention to Nick.

"You never get too far from trouble, do you?" Mike snapped.

Nick smirked. "I'm lucky that way."

"I take it you two know each other," Jacinth said, as the tension between them spiked.

"Too well." Mike let it go at that and scanned the area. "Where's this body part that you claim fell from the wall."

Claim, as if her version were in doubt. "On the floor in the guest bathroom where it fell. Follow me."

She opened the door, pointed at the head and immediately started coughing. The dust had settled in the room like a milky cloud of poisonous smoke. Both Mike and Jordon stepped over the worst of the debris to reach the decomposing body part. Neither she nor Nick crowded into the space with them.

Mike stooped for a closer look. "You have any idea how this got in the walls?"

"Not a clue," Jacinth answered. "The house has been standing since the Civil War."

"The head hasn't been hanging around for nearly that long," Mike quipped.

"How long has it been hanging around?" Jacinth asked.

"Can't say for sure, but my guess is that the victim was living and breathing this time a year ago. We'll get a more accurate estimate from the forensics team."

If the officer was even close to right, the decapitation took place after her grandmother had died or at least after she'd gone to live in the nursing home. It was a relief to know she couldn't have been involved in any way.

The frightening part was that the victim could have been killed in this very house after Jacinth and Caitlyn had inherited it.

"Are you the current owner of the house?" Jordon asked.

"Yes. Well, my sister and I own it together. We inherited it from my grandmother."

"How long have you lived in the house?"

"Eleven months. We'd planned to fix it up and sell it, but then we fell in love with it and decided to stay."

Of course they didn't realize then that it came with spare body parts. Or that the constant repairs needed to keep it livable would drive them to the edge of bankruptcy.

She went over the facts about the inheritance from her grandmother, Marie Villaré.

Jordon made notes. "Did your grandmother live alone prior to moving into the Sunnydale Retirement Center?"

"As far as I know," Jacinth said. "We weren't close. In fact, I hadn't seen her since I was small child."

Mike used the cuff of his shirtsleeve to wipe a smear of dust from the tip of his nose. "Why is that?"

"My mother had issues with my father's family and had severed all ties with them when I was just a toddler."

"Maybe for good reason," Jordon said. "What about your father?"

"He was murdered here in New Orleans over twenty years ago. I don't really remember him."

"How old was Marie Villaré when she died?"

"Seventy."

"Cause of death?"

"She had a heart attack. She'd been diagnosed with coronary problems and diabetes just before moving to the Sunnydale Center."

Jordon continued to stare at the head as Mike stood and stepped away from it.

"Helen Fizelle will have a field day with this one," Jordon said. "Decapitation and missing body parts in a crumbling mansion on the edge of the French Quarter. Right up her alley."

"Who's Helen Fizelle?" Jacinth asked.

"She heads up the skeletal recovery team. Worked with the FBI's Body Farm up in Knoxville a few years back. Nothing she likes better than a case like this."

"You won't have to leave the head here until she can see it, will you?"

"Nah," Mike said, scrunching his mouth into a bizarre shape. "We'll take pictures and then deliver the skeletal remains to Forensic Sciences. The CSU investigation can wait until morning to take a look around, seeing as how the crime scene is already polluted and not how the killer left it."

"But we'll tape off the bathroom," Jordon added. "You'll need to stay out of it and leave things exactly as they are until the detective gives you the okay to clean it up. I'm sure a house this size has plenty of other bathrooms."

"Yes." Unfortunately, none of the other four had been completely remodeled as this one had. One step forward, ten steps back.

"You'll need to close the door and keep that cat out of here, too," Mike added, turning and scowling at Sin, who had crept into the room and scooted beneath the antique claw-foot tub.

"And, of course, the homicide detective assigned to the case will want to question you further."

"Question me about what? I've told you all I know."

Mike ignored the question and avoided eye contact

with her, instead studying the ceiling as if he expected a new rain of additional body parts at any moment.

"Why not have the CSU team come out and investigate tonight?" Nick asked. "They might be able to locate the rest of the body inside the crumbling cavity and hand over all the remains to Helen at once."

"Anything they'll find has been here for months," Mike said. "I don't reckon it's going to deteriorate that more much by morning."

"Just trying to help."

"If I need your help, Bruno, I'll ask for it. Wouldn't stand around waiting if I was you."

Hostility fired like flint between the two men.

Mike pulled a small camera from his shirt pocket.

"Let's give them work room," Jacinth offered in an attempt to keep the peace. She swooped up Sin and she and Nick left the two men alone to take their pictures.

Sin cuddled in her arms for all of a minute before she squirmed her way free and pranced to the door of Marie's old bedroom. Without a look back, the silver-gray Persian disappeared into the dark, antique-filled room that still held the lingering fragrance of lavender.

"What's with you and Officer Friendly?" Jacinth asked as soon as they were out of Mike and Jordon's earshot.

"It's a long story."

"How about the condensed version?"

"We had a run-in a while back."

"About what?"

"His failure to adequately protect the integrity of the evidence in a case I was hired to investigate."

So the conflict between them was at the professional level. That relieved her mind a bit.

"Whatever he does tonight is fine with me," Jacinth said, "as long as the decapitated head leaves with him."

"Not a chance he'll leave that behind," Nick assured her. "The chief would have *his* head."

"Do you think he's right about the approximate date of death?"

"Close. Temperature variances and humidity make it difficult to estimate, but forensics will get a handle on it."

Jacinth stopped on the bottom stair and leaned against the polished mahogany banister. "I really appreciate your coming to my rescue tonight. But I've taken enough of your time. You should get back to your boxes."

"If you're still nervous, I could hang around, have a beer and keep you company until Jordon and Mike are finished."

"I'm fine," she said. And she didn't have a beer in the house.

She walked him to the door. Nick lingered, leaning against the door frame, his gaze locked with hers. Awareness slithered through her, warm and a tad unsettling.

"Thanks again," she whispered, hating that her voice held a throaty rasp. Just the dust, she told herself.

Yet when he leaned in closer, a tingling sensation danced up her spine. Instead of a kiss, he trailed a rough finger down her cheek. "I'm not quite through moving in, but I'm staying in the carriage house tonight. If you need anything at all, just call."

"Thanks. I'll keep that in mind."

She closed and locked the door behind him, leaning against it to regain the equilibrium his touch had destroyed. Seconds later, she stepped to the front window in the stuffy parlor, pulled back the heavy drapes and watched Nick swagger back to his truck.

When he turned toward the house, she stepped away quickly, feeling a bit like she used to when her mother had caught her reading under the sheet with a flashlight long after her bedtime.

The imagery evolved and instead of a book cuddled beneath her sheets, she imagined Nick there. She closed her eyes and willed it away. She had just inherited a whole new set of problems and the last thing she needed was a sexy neighbor she knew absolutely nothing about to complicate matters.

Chapter Three

Nick shucked his jeans and hung them on the back of the antique rocker in his new bedroom. The bedroom was larger than what he was used to, more windows, higher ceilings, newer carpet. And neater. He hadn't had time to litter the place with his newspapers, shoes and dirty clothes yet.

The bed looked comfortable, not that he ever slept soundly or long. He'd be lucky if he got more than a few hours' sleep tonight.

Nothing wrong with the Findleys' carriage house, except that he hated the strangeness, especially when he had a perfectly good house on the Westbank.

But when he'd spotted the Furnished Apartment for Rent sign on the Findleys' front yard, he'd jumped at the chance to rent it. It was perfect for what he needed.

Jacinth's leaky pipe couldn't have fit better with his plans if he'd taken a monkey wrench to it and released the deluge himself. The decapitated head he could have done without.

The last thing he'd expected or needed was a new murder to intersect with the old one. The situation would complicate matters, but at least it had gotten him inside the crumbling mansion and closer to Jacinth. It was a start.

Which was why he couldn't let Jacinth get to him on a personal level.

He just had to remember she was a Villaré. That should be enough to quell any lustful vibes she inspired, as long as he didn't look into those bewitching dark-chocolate eyes of hers.

He shook his head as he threw back the sheet and collapsed onto the bed. Thinking of Jacinth's eyes—or any other of her body parts for that matter—would not help him get to sleep. And he'd have to be up at dawn for the one date he always kept.

A date that would serve as a bitter reminder that Nick was running out of time.

JACINTH WOKE WITH A START as the piercing ring of her cell phone broke through the layers of sleep. She'd lain awake until after four. That seemed only minutes ago, but already slanted rays of sunshine pushed through the half-closed blinds.

Jacinth fumbled for the phone, knocking her paperback novel to the floor. She cringed at the thud. Her head hurt. Her sinuses were clogged. Her mouth was so dry it was difficult to swallow.

She mumbled a hello.

"Jacinth?"

Caitlyn. Jacinth took a deep breath and tried to sound enthusiastic. "What are you doing calling this time of the morning? Don't tell me the honeymoon's grown boring."

"The honeymoon is sheer perfection, and the beach condo we rented has a marvelous view. When the sun hits the water, the Gulf appears striped with the most regal shades of emerald and turquoise I have ever seen."

"Sounds divine."

"It is, and you sound hoarse. Are you coming down with something?"

A case of crumbling drywall overload. Jacinth would have loved to spill the whole story and get her sister's take on last night's gore.

But Caitlyn had been through her own nightmare mere weeks before, barely escaping with her life before she married Marcus. She deserved this period of un-adulterated happiness.

"I feel fine," Jacinth said, "but my allergies are kicking up. Probably some fall-blooming plant we didn't have in Ohio."

"Maybe you should see the doctor."

"I will if it gets worse. Now tell me about the Florida Panhandle. Is the sand really as soft and sugar-white as they say?"

"Absolutely." Caitlyn raved on, excitement and happiness radiating from her voice. Jacinth only half listened, her mind already jumping ahead to the promised visit from a homicide detective and the CSU unit.

And hopefully a visit from the plumber. She needed a shower in the worst way.

As soon as they'd said their goodbyes, Jacinth threw her legs over the side of the bed, tiptoed to the window and stared out at the dew-kissed lawn. The St. Augustine grass was still green and growing in spite of the scattering of leaves that had fallen from the aged live oaks that grew on her and the Findleys' property.

Her gaze moved to the carriage house where Nick had said he'd be if she needed anything at all. A tinge of awareness titillated her senses, just as it had when he'd leaned in so close last night.

It was a schoolgirl response brought on by over-wrought emotions. She did not get giddy over men she barely knew, no matter how helpful and sexy.

At any rate, his promise to be there if she needed him apparently didn't extend to the daylight hours. His truck was gone from the driveway. If he was working, he'd definitely gotten an early start.

She needed to, as well. But first, caffeine. The stairs creaked and groaned as she shuffled down them. When she'd first moved into the house, she'd reacted to every ghostly rasp and moan, thinking someone was behind her.

She thought of them as the whispered secrets of the Villarés who'd lived and died in the house for generations. At least she had until last night. Now she wondered if the walls were merely preparing to drop another body part on her.

And this after the building inspector she'd hired had assured her the foundation was sound and that with loving care and timely repairs the house might stand another hundred and fifty years.

Sin indulged in a kind of purring yowl and walked

to her empty feeding dish as Jacinth stepped into the kitchen.

"I know. Time for breakfast. As if you'd let me forget. My grandmother obviously spoiled you rotten."

From the cabinet Jacinth took a can of the fishy-smelling canned food that Sin loved, opened it and filled the cat's bowl. She gave her fresh water, as well, and then started a full pot of coffee. She had a feeling she'd need it before the day was over.

Her thoughts went back to her grandmother as the enticing odor of brewing coffee filled the cozy kitchen. Marie Villaré had never been a part of Jacinth's life. Jacinth didn't remember one birthday card or phone call from the woman. Her name was never mentioned by Jacinth's mother. Yet the inheritance that Marie Villaré had left Jacinth and Caitlyn served as a golden binding, reaching from beyond the grave to connect Jacinth with her Villaré ancestors and especially with her grandmother.

Yet numerous questions still went unanswered.

Had Marie ever wondered about her granddaughters? Why had she made no attempt to contact them even after their mother had died of cancer? If she had no interest in knowing them, why will them this house?

Had Jacinth's mother left New Orleans because of her husband's murder, or had Marie Villaré done something to cause Sophie to leave Louisiana and never return or even want to speak of the city or this house again?

The phone rang as Jacinth poured her coffee, jerking her back to the present. A drop of hot liquid spilled over her fingers.

"I'm Detective Ron Greene," said the voice on the line as soon as she'd identified herself. "I hear you had a little excitement at your place last night."

"*Shock* might be a better word."

"Yeah. I'm reading the police report now. Some of the details are a little fuzzy. I'll need to talk to you as soon as possible. Do you have any problem with me coming over this morning?"

"No. I'm available anytime."

"Then I'm on my way. The Crime Scene Unit will get there at approximately the same time."

"That will be fine."

The sooner they got this over with the better. Grabbing her coffee cup, Jacinth headed back upstairs to get dressed.

She hesitated a few seconds in front of the closed door to her crime-scene bathroom. Maybe this old house was cursed after all and had stealthily lured Jacinth and Caitlyn into its web of evil.

And maybe Jacinth had been sniffing too much plaster.

She shook off the mood and hurried to get dressed for her own reality CSI.

NICK TOOK THE hard plastic chair in front of the pane of thick glass. As always, this place, with its institutional gray walls, armed and aloof guards and acrid smell of cleansers and sweat, created a hard knot in the depths of his gut.

He'd been ten years old when he'd come here the first time. It was also the first time since he was a first grader that he'd laid eyes on the father he'd been told was out of county on a special mission for his country.

His boyhood superhero instantly dissolved into a flesh-and-blood disillusionment, leaving a hole the size of a bowling ball in his heart.

Nick hadn't said a word to the stranger staring back at him. Finally his mother dragged him back to their old Chevy and he'd thrown up all the way home, soaking the backseat with vomit. His mother had cried hysterically and just kept driving.

He hadn't returned to the prison until he was sixteen years old, two months after his mother had remarried and moved to Pennsylvania, leaving him to live with his paternal grandparents while he finished high school.

The second visit to the prison had been at the urging of his grandfather. No pressure, Gramps had promised. Nick only had to go and make up his own mind if he wanted to engage. If not, they'd leave and nothing would be lost except the morning.

Nick hadn't walked away and the sluggish, agonizing process of building a relationship with his father had begun that day.

Nick watched a woman walk across the floor of the visitor center flanked by two preschoolers. The girl's short ponytail was tied with a bright pink ribbon that matched her shirt. A worn teddy bear with one arm missing was clutched in her right hand.

The boy was tugging at his mother's skirt, as if trying to slow down her progress across the scuffed tile floor. An action figure dangled from his fingers.

Nick swallowed hard, aching for the kids. If they

were here to visit their father, they had a tough road in front of them.

A slight tapping on the window got Nick's attention. His father smiled broadly as if they were meeting for lunch or to go to a Saints game. Nick saw past the smile to the dark bags around his father's sunken eyes, the pall of his complexion and the swollen jowls.

The chemo was doing a number on him.

Nick picked up the phone in front of him. "How you doing, Dad?"

"I'm hanging in there."

"Are they taking care of you?"

"Yep. Dr. Singleton makes sure of that."

Tom Singleton was his oncologist, the one making the decisions on Elton Bruno's medical care. Nick had talked to him by phone a couple of times and checked out his reputation on the internet. He was a well-respected doctor.

That didn't make it any easier for Nick to watch his father go through the treatments knowing they might be in vain and that his father could die in this prison. Knowing he might die waiting for a parole that wouldn't come for a crime Nick was certain his father hadn't committed.

"What's going on with you?" Elton asked. "Any interesting new cases?"

"One. I can't talk about it yet, but when it's solved, I'll feed you all the details."

"Sounds good. Weather's great today. You going fishing when you leave here?"

"Not today."

"Got other plans?"

"Thinking of volunteering to fix a busted pipe for a friend." Unless the plumber had beat him to it.

"A lady friend?"

"How'd you guess?"

"You never liked plumbing when you were working with your grandfather. I figured you had to have some pretty good motivation to make you volunteer your services."

"Not the kind of motivation you're thinking. She's just a neighbor."

"Then you should blow the plumbing off and go fishing. The day is too nice to waste hanging out with rusted metal."

"Good point."

Elton curled his hands around the back of his head and leaned back, balancing his chair on the two back legs as if he didn't have a care in the world. "I'd like to go pole me a pirogue down a lazy bayou and pull in a couple of spiky, mustached old catfish. Fry them right there over an open fire. Down them with a six-pack of cold ones for a chaser while the gators float by and the blue jays squawk overhead."

For most men, that wasn't much to ask. Nick planned to do everything in his power to see that Elton had the chance to live that dream before he died.

"Any word from your attorney on the parole hearing?"

"I'm nowhere near the top of the list. But if I do get out of here, we're going to take that fishing trip."

"I'll be ready," Nick said.

"I want me some boiled crawfish, too. Some days I can almost smell them." Elton smiled. "Course it always turns out it's just the spices in the heartburn chow I'm smelling."

Elton sat up straight again. "You know what else I'd like?"

"Why don't you tell me?"

"To touch a woman, a real woman with curves and soft skin and hair that smells like flowers in springtime. You know the kind of woman I'm talking about?"

An image of Jacinth slipped into Nick's consciousness. A Villaré—of all people to think of here in this place. "Yeah, I know the kind of woman you mean. They usually spell trouble."

"Just a thought," Elton said, this time chuckling into the phone. "Hell, even if I had a woman like that I probably couldn't get it up with all this chemo they're shooting into me."

Probably not the best place to go with this conversation. "Did you give any more thought to what I asked you about last time I was here?" Nick asked.

Elton rubbed his jaw as all sign of his forced smile vanished.

"I've thought about it for the last twenty-two years. I've come up with a thousand different theories about who might have killed Micah, but none of them holds water. Truth is, with all the scenarios I've considered, I don't even trust my memories any longer. But it's all in the trial notes."

Notes that Nick had been over a thousand times before and gotten nowhere with. But the trial had been manipulated by lawyers and layered with rules, objections and emotions. Truth could get tangled up in that.

"Just think about it again, Dad."

"It won't help. I don't have anything new to tell you, son. I wish I did."

But Nick was not about to give up, not while his father had a breath left in his cancer-wracked body.

Someone had gotten away with murder and his father was paying for the crime. He had a good idea who that someone was.

But he needed more than supposition. He needed proof. That's where Jacinth came in.

RON GREENE WOULD NEVER be cast as the lead on a TV detective show. His face was pocked and treaded, likely the result of teenage acne gone mad and apparently untreated. His scowl was perpetual, the lines in his brow permanent, the wrinkles deeply furrowed though he was probably no more than mid-fifties.

But he definitely had that detective air about him, authoritative and intimidating. Even Sin had gone into hiding when he showed up.

That was two hours ago. Now the CSU was done and gone, leaving Ron Greene time to focus all his attention on Jacinth.

Just looking into his piercing eyes inspired guilt and gave her a compelling desire to confess something. The worst offense she could think of was running a yellow light on her way to work last Tuesday. She doubted the detective would be impressed.

She led him to the kitchen for the interrogation, or

chat as he referred to it. The parlor with its uncomfortable antique seating seemed a poor fit for his six-foot-plus frame. The den seemed too cozy.

He turned down her offer of coffee and asked for water as he dropped into one of the kitchen chairs. "Mind if I tape our conversation?" he asked.

"No, why would I?"

"No reason, but I'm required to ask." He took a small recorder from his shirt pocket, set it on the table in front of him and pushed a button.

A green light flashed and suddenly she grew nervous, though she wasn't sure why. It wasn't as if he could possibly consider her a suspect. Or could he?

Nonetheless, she was only telling the truth and that wouldn't change. So why worry that it was being taped?

"Some of this is in the police report," the detective said, "but I'll have you restate it for my records."

She nodded.

"Will you state your full name and age?"

"Jacinth Elizabeth Villaré. I'm twenty-four years old."

"Single?"

"Yes."

"How long have you lived at this address?"

"Eleven months." She went over the details of the inheritance once again—explaining how she and Caitlyn had come down to New Orleans from Ohio with the intention of picking up the keys from the estate attorney and listing the house with a real estate company.

"What made you decide to stay?" Greene asked.

Admitting they'd fallen in love with the house and

felt it was calling to them sounded far too corny to share with the blunt detective. "We found the city intriguing and Tulane University offered the graduate program I was looking for."

"What program would that be?"

"American Cultural History."

"It says in the police report that you work at Tulane."

"I have a teaching assistantship while I complete my doctorate. I don't see how these questions are going to help you find out what happened to the woman who lost her head."

"I'm just trying to get a timeline here. What I'm going to need from you are the names of anyone who had access to the house after it was deeded to you. Construction workers, friends, cleaning staff, anyone who had a key or had one in his possession long enough to have one made."

"I'll have to give that some thought." Unfortunately, there had been a constant stream of workers in those first few weeks after she and Caitlyn had moved in.

"I'd like to have the list by tonight. You can always add names later as you think of them. I'll give you my card and you can fax the names to me."

"Okay."

"And I'm going to need as much information as I can get on your late grandmother's lifestyle. Names of her caretakers. Whether or not she had renters or frequent visitors. Names of her friends."

"I won't be much help to you there. I didn't have a relationship with my grandmother. The last contact I had with her was when I was two years old."

Detective Greene shot her a look of undisguised skepticism. "So how did you get in the will?"

"My best guess is that my sister and I are the only living relatives she had left. I can't swear to that, though."

He clicked his tongue against the roof of his mouth and raked his fingers through his thinning hair. "Your knowing nothing about the house before you moved in will complicate the investigation," he said, his expression suggesting she'd let him down.

"What about letters, diaries, old photos? Your grandmother must have left some of those around the house."

"Not that we've located."

"See what you can find."

"I've already searched the closets and the attic and every place else she might have kept personal information. I didn't find anything except some old receipts and Post-it notes she had stuck on half the surfaces in the house."

Jacinth smiled as she remembered her grandmother's haphazard method of organizing. "They were mostly reminders of appointments and to take her meds."

"What kind of appointments?"

"Doctors. Hair. Nails. Gladys Findley said she was very concerned about her appearance right up until the end."

"Who's Gladys Findley?"

"My next-door neighbor." She nodded toward the window with a view of the Findley house.

"Do you still have the notes?"

"No. They didn't seem important." Jacinth rearranged herself in the chair and met the detective's steely gaze. She had a few questions of her own and this seemed as good a time as any to ask them. "Do you have a definitive answer for how long the victim had been dead?"

"Not yet."

"An ID?"

"No. She's still labeled the Jane Doe head."

"What about the search you just made of my bathroom?"

"What about it?"

"Did you find any more skeletal remains?"

"This is a police matter now. I'm not at liberty to discuss specifics of the evidence."

"It's my house. I have a right to know if there are bodies inside my walls."

"As far as I can tell, you're clear of corpses."

She sighed, relieved. "Does that mean I can start repairing the room?"

"I'd hold off on structural repairs in case we need to investigate further. You could go ahead and have the plumbing checked out and also the roof. You seem to have a leak somewhere. The walls are wet from the inside out."

"I will." As soon as she could afford it. That might not be anytime soon.

"Has anything like this ever happened before?" she asked.

"Women decapitated?"

"No, bodies or body parts found inside houses in this area?"

"Not recently. Until I get a complete autopsy report, we don't even know if the victim was alive or dead when the decapitation took place. It could be a sick prank, teenagers stealing bodies from the cemetery and conducting their own science experiments."

"The neighbors haven't mentioned any teenagers living in this house."

"No, but they could have had access to it during the time it was empty."

The detective turned off his recorder and returned it to his pocket as he stretched to a standing position. "You can relax," the detective said, offering his first attempt at empathy. "I don't think you're in any danger, Ms. Villaré. But use caution. Don't open your door to strangers or get involved with people you know nothing about. I would advise that even if we hadn't found the partial remains of Jane Doe. You can't be too careful these days."

She preached that same thing herself and yet she'd opened her door to Nick last night. Thankfully, he'd just been a helpful neighbor, one she'd likely never see again.

A man would have to be crazy to get involved with this mess. She walked out to the porch with the detective as he was leaving. No sign of Nick's truck. He was probably staying as far away from her as possible.

Who could blame him?

JACINTH LUGGED THE LAST TWO bags from the car to the kitchen. Considering that Caitlyn and Marcus were in Florida and Jacinth spent most of her waking hours at the university, it was ridiculous how many groceries she'd bought.

She tackled putting away the refrigerator items first, pretty sure just handling the carton of chocolate-fudge ice cream added a few inches to her hips. Had she not been in the frozen-treat aisle when the plumber had returned her call, she could have resisted the fattening splurge.

It would be Monday afternoon before he could get to the busted water pipe so that she could have running water again. That meant she'd have to drive over to the university to wash her hair and shower in the gym facilities.

The yogurt and skim milk were staples, as were her fruit, granola, cheese, salad makings and an assortment of canned and boxed soups. And she'd stocked up on Prissy Whiskers, the only cat food Sin deemed flavorsome enough for her majesty's taste buds.

The beer was another story. She didn't drink it. She knew nothing about it. Nonetheless, she'd picked up two six-packs, one imported, one domestic. It took some creative rearranging in her fridge to make room for them.

Not that there was any reason to expect her hunky neighbor would drop by for a visit, although his truck was in the driveway now.

Not that she cared. She wasn't the least bit infatuated by him.

Kicking out of her shoes at the foot of the stairs, she went upstairs to work on her list for the detective and see why Sin was making such a racket. The pitiful meowing grew louder as Jacinth reached the top step.

"Sin, what are you into now?"

There was no sign of the cat, but the mewing turned to an earsplitting howl now that Sin had an audience. Jacinth searched for her without luck until she realized that the wail was coming from behind the closed door of Marie's old bedroom.

Jacinth opened the door and Sin instantly grew quiet. The feline sat perfectly still, nailing Jacinth with her menacing yellow-eyed stare as if she were the culprit. Jacinth stooped to pick her up.

"You did this to yourself, Sin, though I can't imagine how you got the door shut tight. And you've made a mess of this room."

The books and framed pictures that lined the shelves were askance. One book was on the floor. So was a shattered vase that Jacinth would have sworn was too heavy for the cat to budge.

She sniffed as an unfamiliar scent assaulted her nostrils. "Did you spill something, Sin? Naughty cat."

Jacinth searched but couldn't find the source of the odor. Yet it persisted. A bit nauseating. Similar to the cheap aftershave one of her students apparently used in lieu of deodorant.

The smell had not been in this room before. Her chest constricted, making it difficult to breathe. Had someone been in the room while she was out?

Taking a deep breath, she carried Sin out of the room and shut the door behind her. Her nerves were shot. She was overreacting. There had been half a dozen CSU professionals in her house this morning. Their scents probably mingled and lingered and only seemed stronger in Marie's room because it had been shut up.

Her doorbell rang and Jacinth jumped as if she'd been poked with a sharp fork. She wasn't expecting company. Sin hissed and wiggled from her grasp, jumping from her arms to the floor.

Jacinth hurried down the stairs and peeked through the peephole. It was Nick. She threw open the door and stared for a few seconds, taking him in, right down to the metal toolbox he held in his right hand.

His jeans were worn, frayed at the hem, ripped across his left thigh. His T-shirt was faded, the fit tight across his broad, muscular chest, the short sleeves rolled up.

Totally lacking in sophistication.

Sex appeal out the wazoo.

"Heard you need a plumber," he said. His smile lit up his face. "Unless you've already been serviced."

Her senses vibrated. "I haven't been serviced, but can I afford you?"

"I'm sure we can work something out."

"In that case, when can you start?"

Chapter Four

A little more than an hour and a half later, Nick rang the doorbell again. This time his shirt was smeared with mud and he was wiping his face on a red work rag.

"Pipe's replaced," he said. "Turn a faucet on and let it run for a few minutes to get any residue out of the system."

"Where did you get the new pipe?"

"The hardware store. Traffic's light today, so it was a quick trip."

She pushed the door open. "Thanks. I'll write you a check to cover the cost."

"We'll settle up later."

"Come on in, while I give the plumbing a try."

"I'd track mud with every step. I'll wait here."

"Then at least let me bring you a beer."

He grinned. "Now you're talking."

Feeling a tad smug that her purchase had not been a waste, she hurried to the kitchen, turned the water on full blast and let it pour into the sink. By the time she'd opened the beer, the flow was running clear. She owed Nick big-time.

The beer would have to suffice for now. Halfway back to the front of the house, she decided this called for a celebration. Returning to the kitchen, she opened a beer for herself and headed back to the porch.

Nick took his long-necked bottle and propped himself against the banister. Jacinth settled on the top step.

"I'm impressed with your skills," she said.

"You should be. I learned from my grandpa, the best darn plumber in Grosse Tete, Louisiana."

"That's a town?"

"Yep. We've even got a truck stop. Be really nice and I might take you there for dinner one night."

Jacinth tapped her chest with her hand. "Be still, my heart." She took another sip of her beer. Not as good as a glass of chardonnay, but not bad. "Actually, I should treat you to dinner tonight. How about burgers at Snug Harbor?"

"Sounds great, but you're not getting off that light. I have a better idea how you can repay me for my labor."

Tension swelled. Surely he wasn't suggesting sexual favors.

"Help me unpack my kitchen items and I'll grill you a steak."

A blush heated her cheeks and she hoped he hadn't read her thoughts. "I'd be glad to help. I'll need a shower first and I have to finish a list I'm preparing for Detective Greene."

"Ron Greene, in Homicide?"

"Yes. I guess you know him, too."

Nick nodded. "Yeah. He can be obnoxious when it

suits him, but he's one of the best at getting his man—or woman. What are you listing?"

Jacinth told him and started to recount her discussion with the detective.

"Looks like you have more company," Nick said, his gaze moving past her.

"Am I interrupting anything?"

Jacinth shifted and turned to find Gladys Findley standing at the end of her walk. "No," she assured her neighbor. "Join us. Your new tenant just repaired my broken water pipe."

"So that's why your lawn is soaked," Gladys said. Her eyebrows arched. "Do you two know each other?"

"We didn't until he came to my rescue last night and turned off my main water valve."

"What a nice gesture," Gladys said.

Gladys was slender with graying hair that—along with her makeup—was always impeccable. Today she wore brown pants and a pale blue sweater that complemented her deep-set eyes.

"I understand you're having some other problems, as well," Gladys said, her voice tentative, as if she hated to broach the subject. "You called the police."

"Yes." Jacinth searched in vain for a delicate way to say that a woman's head had fallen out of her wall.

"Detective Greene came to see me today," Gladys said, not waiting for Jacinth's account. "He told me what happened. You must have been terrified."

"Yes, evidently you missed my banshee scream."

"We were out last night. Paul had gotten us tickets to the symphony."

"Lucky you. Fortunately for me, Nick was around. He came running and stayed with me until the police arrived."

Gladys turned her gaze toward Nick. "Not even completely moved in yet, and already you're proving to be quite the heroic addition to our neighborhood."

"I try to make a good first impression." Nick stood and walked over to Gladys. "Exactly what did the detective have to say when he came to see you?"

"He questioned me about Marie Villaré's friends."

"What did you tell him?"

"That I didn't really know Marie all that well. We spoke when we were both in the yard, but I'm ashamed to admit I had never even been inside the Villaré house until the week Marie was moving out. She invited me over then to ask if I'd look after her cat until her granddaughters arrived. That was the first I'd heard about Jacinth and Caitlyn."

"Did you notice people coming and going from the house?" Jacinth asked.

"No. Marie seldom entertained guests and never family, at least that I knew of. I did know about her stepson who was murdered, but only because his ex-girlfriend still came around occasionally. If she saw me outside, she always stopped to talk."

"It was my father who was murdered," Jacinth corrected. "Micah Villaré, a son, not a stepson. He was killed when I was very young, and he was married to my mother at the time. I can't imagine one of his old girlfriends still coming around."

Gladys shook her head. "The girlfriend never mentioned a Micah. She only mentioned Luther and I'm sure she said he was Marie's stepson and that he'd been killed three years ago while on a hunting trip in Alaska. It may be more like four years now, since it's been a while since she told me about his death."

If a stepson named Luther existed, Jacinth had never heard of him. No big surprise. There was much about the Villarés that she didn't know. She'd have to find a way to remedy that.

"Anyway, I forgot to mention the girlfriend to the detective," Gladys said. "I don't know how close they were, but I know she came over and helped Marie move into the nursing facility."

"What's her name?" Nick asked.

"The first name was Carrie. I remember because I have a granddaughter named that. I think the last name was Marks, but I wouldn't swear to it."

"I'll be in contact with the detective," Jacinth said. "I'll be glad to give him the name for you."

"I'd appreciate that. I wish I could be more help, but I'm not the most social of neighbors and Marie was a very private person."

"Losing two sons to murder might make you that way," Jacinth said. And then Marie had lost her only daughter-in-law and her two granddaughters. More than ever, Jacinth wondered about the story behind that.

She was certain that the rejection had been provoked. Sophie Villaré had been a fantastic mother and Jacinth had never known her to be vengeful.

They talked for a few minutes more before Gladys wandered back across the lawns. But Jacinth had paid little attention to the rest of the conversation. Her concentration was on coming to grips with the situation and taking control.

She knew what she had to do. Tonight, after dinner, she'd be the one offering a proposition to Nick.

THERE WAS AMAZINGLY LITTLE unpacking to do. Nick's kitchen equipment consisted of the bare necessities to prepare and serve a simple meal, but little else. A few pans, a set of crockery dishes, some very sharp knives and a set of mismatched flatware.

But the apartment was charming, the furnishings provided by the Findleys an eclectic blend of authentic antiques and what appeared to be renovated yard-sale finds.

Jacinth especially loved the kitchen with its French-style windows with swing-open sashes. The delicate curtains were in a flowered, provincial pattern. The range and refrigerator were modern, but the acacia wood French bistro dining set oozed old-world charm.

Too bad the dilapidated carriage house on the back of the Villaré property had been neglected for so long. They could have used the extra money a tenant would have brought in.

As it was, she wasn't even sure the rickety structure was safe to enter and was surprised the city hadn't insisted it be torn down. Likely the only reason they hadn't was that the eyesore wasn't visible from the street. Nick had lucked out finding a place this comfortable and quaint.

Jacinth was glad she'd thought to bring a bottle of

wine for his first dinner in his new apartment. He'd served it in water glasses along with a melt-in-your-mouth fillet and a simple salad of fresh greens and avocado. The informality suited Nick's personality to a T.

They lingered at the table after the meal, talking and sipping the pinot noir she'd been saving for a special occasion. This definitely qualified. She hadn't enjoyed a man's company this much in years, if ever.

Nick was funny and fascinating and she'd completely let down her guard with him, which was totally unlike her and probably not the best idea since she knew so little about him.

Jacinth knew she was usually somewhat standoffish around strangers. Some considered her downright stuffy. Her sister pointed that out to her on a regular basis. But she was a doctoral student, a future history professor. Could she help it if she acted like one?

Still, she'd like to be more outgoing and less afraid of new adventures—and of relationships. The last man she'd dated had complained she was cold.

He was wrong. She had heat. She was just waiting for the right man to light her fire.

"You travel light," she said. "Or do you still have more belongings to move?"

"I have a few more boxes, mostly books and fishing gear. I'm a low-maintenance kind of guy."

Or maybe he'd just broken up with a girlfriend or wife. That would explain his needing a furnished place and bringing so little with him. But what woman would be crazy enough to let him go?

"Where did you live before renting the carriage house?" she asked.

"On the Westbank."

"Which is actually the East bank of the Mississippi River," she said. "Or so a colleague explained it."

"He's right. The river forms a crescent as it flows through the city so directions get confusing."

"Did you live alone?"

"You're just full of questions tonight."

"Just trying to figure you out."

He leaned back in his chair. "I'm not that complicated. And, yes, I lived alone."

"Have you ever been married?"

"Nope. I came close once, but she came to her senses and left me for an NFL linebacker. He's since left her, and she married their divorce attorney."

"That must have devastated you."

His lips parted in a slightly crooked smile that sent her pulse racing.

"The Saints not making the playoffs would leave me devastated," he said. "Getting dumped by Janice for a rich jock pissed me off."

She pushed her glass aside. "Then you probably deserved to get left."

"No doubt about it. We were in lust, not love. I may have missed out on the love gene. How about you? Is there some guy who'd be fiercely jealous knowing I'm sitting across the table from you tonight and totally infatuated by the way your eyes sparkle beneath those incredible lashes?"

Warmth flushed her body and left a burn in her cheeks. "Not likely."

"You're much too modest. New Orleans men aren't stupid. I'm sure you're hit on regularly by students and professors."

She smiled and offered an exaggerated batting of her eyes. "Maybe a few." None as sexy or as exciting as Nick.

Nick finished his wine. "There's a full moon tonight. How about we take a walk so that you can acquaint me with my new neighborhood?"

"I'd like that." And it would give her even more time to decide how to phrase her proposition.

The night was mildly cool, the wind just strong enough to occasionally blow wisps of hair into Jacinth's face. She pulled her ruby-colored cardigan tighter as she and Nick fell into an easy rhythm.

Jacinth had walked these streets many times, but always in the daytime and usually at a power-walk pace. Moonlight transformed the aging mansions along the wide avenue, making them appear much grander, more welcoming.

Features that had gone unnoticed before captured her attention. An intricate grapevine pattern in an iron gate. The twisted trunk of an aged oak tree. A storefront window etched in gold with a hand-painted border of magnolia blossoms.

And all of it mingling with the almost giddy feeling of awareness that Nick invoked. Their shoulders brushed and he linked his hand with Jacinth's.

Her breath caught and held. She swallowed hard,

determined not to let her emotions get out of hand. Still, feeling anything at all for Nick seemed crazy. They were virtual strangers.

"Nice area," Nick commented. "I can see why you and your sister decided to keep the house even with all the work it needs."

"There is an exuberance for life here I've never found anywhere else. The inhabitants love their food, their music, their traditions, and take advantage of any reason to celebrate."

"Your mother obviously didn't share your appreciation for New Orleans, since she never brought you and your sister back for a visit."

"She had issues."

"Related to her husband's murder?"

Jacinth hesitated, the nagging questions that had been on her mind all day causing her to tense. She seldom talked to anyone except Caitlyn about her mother's New Orleans mania, but if she was going to ask for Nick's help, she might as well level with him.

"Anything I say would be based on conjecture. Mother refused to talk about the murder, her life here or about our father's family. It was if she'd locked that part of her life up in a soundproof and airtight container and dropped it so deep in the Gulf it could never surface."

"And she never mentioned the murder?"

"When we were very young, she told us our daddy had died in a fishing accident. It wasn't until I was ten years old and badgering her with questions about my father and his family that she explained he'd been murdered."

"That was all she told you about it?"

"That was it. I could see how even saying that much upset her, so both Caitlyn and I decided it best to let it go."

"Was she that way with other problems?"

"On the contrary. She never backed down from anything or anyone, especially if it involved what she thought was best for Caitlyn and me. No one could have asked for a better mother."

"A tiger, huh?"

"If it was called for. But she was also loving, fun and enthusiastic."

Nick grew quiet again and she withdrew into her own thoughts as they crossed Esplanade and took a side street into the densely populated Faubourg Marigny neighborhood.

Another turn landed them on Frenchmen Street. Music drifted from a small jazz club on the next corner. Patrons spilled onto the sidewalk, drinks in the familiar to-go cups in hand.

Nick stopped at the edge of a cluster of college-aged partiers and slipped his arm around Jacinth's waist. "Would you like to stop and have a drink?"

"The two glasses of wine I drank at your place were more than enough for me. If you'd like one, I'll go in with you. The music sounds good."

"I can do without it." He pulled her close. "You're about as intoxicating as I can handle, Jacinth Villaré."

He swayed to the rhythm, his hard body pressing

against hers. Her stomach quivered as she gave in to the thrill of the moment. Who knew dancing in the moonlight could be so deliciously erotic?

"Hey there, hottie." The blaring, slurred voice shattered the mood.

Jacinth looked up just as someone fell hard against her, his elbow jabbing her just above her right ear. His drink spilled down the front of her blouse as he grabbed hold of her shoulder.

Nick simultaneously steadied her and caught the man in a stranglehold. His flexed muscles pressed against the sleeves of his shirt. His expression in the shadowed caverns of light escaping the bar was so intense it frightened Jacinth.

"I'm okay, Nick," she insisted. "It was just an accident."

"Getcha hands off me," the man slurred. "I's just want my turn dancin' with the chick." Spittle or maybe whiskey dribbled from the corner of his mouth.

Nick exhaled slowly and loosed the stranglehold, replacing it with a hand tightly clasped around the intoxicated man's arm. "You're drunk and you almost knocked the lady's head off."

An older man exited the bar, saw what was going on and rushed over. He wrapped an arm around the drunk's shoulders but locked gazes with Nick. "Is Seth giving you trouble?"

"Ask her." Nick nodded toward Jacinth. "She's the one who got hit in the head and soaked in his whiskey."

"I'm okay," Jacinth repeated. "Really, I'm fine."

"I'm sorry," the older guy said. "Seth gets a little

rambunctious when he's under the influence. I didn't mean to let him go off on his own. He walked out while I was paying for drinks."

"You need to get him home," Nick said.

"Yeah. I will." He led the staggering Seth away.

"Are you sure you're okay?" Nick asked.

"I'm sure, though I may smell like a brewery." And she was still stunned by Nick's razor-sharp defense instincts and not certain if she should feel protected or apprehensive.

"Where did you pick that up?" she asked.

"What?"

"You had poor Seth in your vise grip before I even fully grasped the situation."

"Training. I was an undercover agent with the CIA for a few years. I infiltrated a cell of terrorists. One mistake with them and they make death seem like a luxury."

That explained the killer reflexes. "A nice line of work to be out of."

"I thought so—after I almost wound up as fish bait in the bottom of a muddy river. Besides, I wasn't much use to the CIA once I'd been identified."

That seemed the perfect lead-in for her purposes. "I'd like to hire you, Nick."

"To fix your pipes or to protect you from clumsy, aggressive drunks?"

"As a private investigator. I'd like to find out as much as I can about my grandmother."

"Don't you think Ron Greene will do that for you?"

"He might, but that doesn't mean he'll share it with me."

"Good point."

"It's a business arrangement, Nick. I'll pay you. Maybe not all at once—I'm a little short on cash at the moment—but I'll get the money."

"If this is because you think Marie Villaré was connected to the murder of the decapitated woman, you're probably way off base."

"My curiosity didn't stem from that, but the mutilation does add urgency to learning about my father's family and what Caitlyn and I have moved into."

The interest stemmed from the secrets that had shaped Jacinth's past. Secrets that seemed alternately terrifying and mesmerizing. Secrets that had driven her mother to leave New Orleans and never speak of it again.

"Then exactly what is it you think I'll find with this investigation?" Nick asked.

"Who my father really was and what kind of family he'd come from. I'd like to know about my father's stepbrother whom I didn't know existed until today."

"And what if I find out he was a sorry son of a bitch who probably got what he deserved? Are you going to want to kill the messenger?"

"I can handle the truth. I'm thinking you could start by talking to Carrie Marks, if you can find her."

"Most people are fairly easy to locate unless they don't want to be found."

"I wouldn't think Carrie's in hiding if she visited Marie at home."

"Carrie's an ex-girlfriend and exes are never reliable character witnesses. Depending on her relationship with Luther, she'll either give you a glowing report on him or tell you he's a scumbag."

"I'll weigh her opinions with others. I'd also like to know how she felt about my grandmother, Marie Villaré."

"Sounds easy enough. I'll get on it."

"Here's the catch, Nick."

"You want it by yesterday."

"I want to be directly involved in your investigation. Once you locate Carrie, I want to be there when you question her."

"Sounds as if you're looking for a facilitator, not a private investigator."

"You'll be doing the investigating. I'll be observing and assessing."

"Observing and assessing sound like terms that came right out of one of your lectures."

"What's wrong with that?"

"Like it or not, any investigation of your family now starts off with a mutilated body. Word will get out that you discovered evidence of a likely murder. You start poking around in the wrong places and the killer's not going to like it."

"I won't be *poking*. I just want to talk to a few people who knew my father's family."

Nick exhaled slowly and then reached for her hand. "Okay, we'll try it your way at first. If I sense you're in any kind of danger, the agreement's off. And I need to caution you like I do all my clients."

"About what?"

"I'm not saying this will be the case in this instance, but sometimes the truth is the last thing you want to hear."

"I'll take that chance."

Neither of them spoke again until they climbed the steps to her house. She considered inviting Nick in for a nightcap, but decided against it. The internal fire that had ignited when he'd pressed his body against hers still smoldered. Best not to fan the flames.

She slipped her key into her lock. "Thanks again," she murmured, "for the rescue last night, the repaired pipe and the steaks."

"My pleasure."

He pressed his right hand against the door frame and leaned in closer. She struggled for breath and some mental clarity. "I'll write you a check tomorrow—for the pipe and an initial payment so that you can get started with the investigation."

"Then you'd be screwing around with my hang-up. I never lend or take money from friends."

"We've just met, Nick. I like you, but we're barely acquaintances. We're definitely not friends."

"Aren't we?"

His lips were mere inches from hers. She knew he was going to kiss her, knew she should turn and retreat inside the house before it went that far. Instead, she rose to her tiptoes and met his lips head-on.

Desire rocked through her and she opened her mouth, meeting the thrust of his tongue, as her body arched toward him. The kiss deepened and the last remnants of inhibition vanished.

When Nick pulled away, her equilibrium was so off-kilter, she could barely keep her balance.

His finger trailed her cheek and he pushed a strand of hair behind her ear. "Lock your door and call if you need me."

She nodded, not sure she could speak. She needed him now, but not for protection.

He shoved his hands into his pockets and backed away from the door. "I'll call you when I have something to report about Carrie."

Back to business, only she was still reeling from the kiss. She nodded again and then managed a shaky good-night before turning away and stepping inside.

Her mind was whirring with sensuous thoughts of Nick as she climbed the winding staircase, but by the time she reached the second floor, reality had pushed its way into her brain.

Reacting with that kind of passion to a man she'd only met yesterday wasn't wise. Hadn't she cautioned Caitlyn with that same advice when she fell so hard and so fast for Marcus?

Okay, so it had worked for Caitlyn. But that didn't mean Jacinth could defy the odds.

Nonetheless, memories of dancing with Nick delivered a disturbing flush of warmth as she washed her face, brushed her teeth and slipped into a pair of flowered, cotton pajamas.

Jacinth looked for Sin and found her curled up asleep near the door to the second-floor veranda. Moonbeams filtered through the French doors, dappling Sin and the walls with silver sequins.

Jacinth opened the door and stepped outside for one last look at the full moon. Perhaps she should blame her overactive hormones on that.

Pulling her hair up and off her neck, she let the wind cool her skin and hopefully tamp down the flickers of desire that still haunted her.

As she turned to go back inside, she spotted a man from the periphery of her vision. He was leaning against the trunk of a tree in front of her neighbors' B and B, a lit cigarette dangling from his mouth. Most likely a paying guest. Ernest and Henry provided lodging in their historic home but didn't allow smoking.

She couldn't see the man's eyes, but his stare was obviously focused in her direction. He put a hand up as if to acknowledge that they were watching each other and then started walking toward her house.

Apprehension prickled her skin, leftover paranoia from last night's incident with the collapsed wall. A minute later, the man snuffed out his smoke with the toe of his shoe and picked up his pace. He walked past her house without looking her way again.

Jacinth went back inside, carefully locking the door behind her. She needed sleep. Peaceful sleep with no nightmares of falling heads or dangerous strangers. And no lustful dreams of Nick.

JACINTH WOKE ON SUNDAY morning to a world shrouded in thick, gray fog and a cold, misty rain. She was quickly learning that drastic and sometimes violent weather changes were the hallmark of a Louisiana autumn.

Somber was an appropriate backdrop for tackling the massive and depressing cleanup job in the guest bathroom. Not that she could repair the walls by herself, but she could at least clean up the disgusting debris.

Before she started on that, she needed her caffeine fix and Sin was likely already in the kitchen, impatiently waiting on breakfast. There was also the matter of broken glass in Marie's bedroom. She was yet to clean that up from yesterday.

Jacinth unfurled herself from bed and slid her bare feet into her slippers. Her gaze unwittingly slid to the window that overlooked the Findleys' carriage house.

Impulsively she touched the tips of her fingers to her lips. If Nick were as good at investigating as he was at kissing, she'd soon know everything about the Villarés.

Nick's truck was parked in the driveway. The temptation to invite him over for morning coffee skittered through her mind. She promptly rejected the idea before her libido could chime in.

Twenty minutes later, her second mug of sweetened coffee in hand and dressed in her favorite faded work jeans, Jacinth stepped into her grandmother's bedroom. The dark mahogany furniture paired with the thick crimson drapes made the room seem dark and desolate.

Evidently, Marie had liked it that way. The entire house had been dark and dreary when Caitlyn and she had moved in. They'd replaced the heavy drapes in almost every room and put splashes of color everywhere.

Jacinth picked up the largest piece of the broken vase, careful to avoid the splintered edges. As she dropped it into the heavy plastic trash bag, she noticed an inscription on what had been the bottom of the vase. Gingerly, she recovered the jagged glass from the bag and turned it over.

Happy Birthday, Mommy.

Love, Micah

Jacinth dropped to the side of the four-poster bed, so excited and moved that her hands were shaking. The father she couldn't even remember had held this vase when he was just a boy growing up in this sprawling mansion. It had been a gift to his mommy—given with love.

Jacinth laid the engraved fragment aside and continued removing shards of glass from the worn Persian rug. When that was finished, she walked to the bookcase and scanned the shelves.

As many times as she'd walked by that vase, she'd never noticed the inscription until it was broken. She may have overlooked other treasures as well.

One shelf was filled with a matching collection of leather-bound copies of the classics. She picked up *To Kill a Mockingbird* and thumbed through it, looking for personal marks or notes in the margins. The pages were pristine.

Next Jacinth chose one of the books that Sin had knocked askance during her lockup tangent. It was in the same type of leather binding as the one she'd just glanced through, but she didn't recognize the title as a classic.

She opened it to find a well-worn copy of a family Bible tucked inside the leather.

Adrenaline surged as she flicked past pages until she found what she'd spent months searching for. A family tree, completely filled in and dating back to the mid-1800s.

Handling the aging Bible with utmost care, Jacinth hurried back to her well-lit bedroom and settled in the rocker near the window. After the incident with the head and learning of the existence of a phantom stepson, she doubted anything she discovered from the family records would shock her.

She was wrong.

Chapter Five

Nick spent the early hours of Sunday morning on the phone with a new client who was convinced that one of his employees was stealing from him. It was a small operation, twenty employees, five of them relatives of the owner. If Nick had to place a bet today, he'd wager the thief—if there was one—would turn out to be one of the relatives.

Nick listened and interacted appropriately, but his real concern this morning was Jacinth and the way she was getting to him. His goal had been to spend time with her and pick her brain about what she'd learned from her mother about Micah's murder. It had not been to get turned on by Jacinth.

Falling for Jacinth would undermine the most important investigation of his life. Yet he was falling and falling hard.

It wasn't just the physical attraction, though that was dynamite. It was the way she talked, the way she smiled, the way she walked, the way she sipped her wine.

Hell, it was everything about her.

He felt this fierce need to protect her, but the one she

needed protection from most was him. He couldn't keep his hands off her. And that kiss last night had equaled the thrill of having sex with any other woman he'd ever been with. Pulling away and leaving her at the door had been downright painful.

None of that changed what he had to do, but he couldn't be lover and destroyer. He'd have to put the skids on any romantic involvement and keep this strictly platonic.

His mind understood and accepted that. His body was the traitor.

Nick spent the rest of the morning following the paper trail and gathering information on Carrie, real name Corinthia Louella Marks. She currently resided in Westwego, across the Crescent City Connection and then about a thirty-minute drive out the Westbank Expressway. Nick knew the area well.

Carrie was thirty-eight years old, never been married, and was renting the house she lived in.

She had two credit cards with a total debt of under five thousand dollars and she drove a six-year-old Chrysler minivan. She worked in an elementary school cafeteria. He'd gotten all the facts, but he knew nothing of who she really was or what she was about.

Nick didn't have to do a search on Luther Villaré. Though he hadn't admitted it to Jacinth when Luther's name came up, he knew all about the illegitimate son of Marie's husband Nathanial.

Luther was a low-down, sorry excuse for humanity. He'd have been the first one Nick suspected of burying the head inside the walls of the Villaré home if the guy hadn't been dead for years.

Nick scrambled a couple of eggs, fried a few slices of bacon and toasted some wheat bread that had grown stale. He took that and a fresh cup of coffee to the most comfortable chair in the small living area so that he could catch the NFL pregame show on ESPN while he ate.

His mind sidetracked the game predictions and reverted to Jacinth. His gut feeling was that he should make an executive decision to ignore her wishes and go talk to Carrie on his own. Then he could dig for facts his way without the rules of engagement he'd have to follow with Jacinth along.

He debated that while he showered, shaved and dressed. Then, despite feeling guilty as hell, he decided to follow his instincts and go alone to see Carrie.

The mist had turned into a steady downpour by the time he made a run for his truck. Halfway out the driveway, he spotted Jacinth backing out of her garage. She saw him, waved and kept going.

Wherever she was off to, she seemed in a hurry to get there—and in a pouring rain. His detective instincts kicked in. Timing was everything.

JACINTH TURNED ON THE HEAT in the car though she wasn't sure the chill she felt had anything to do with the temperature. Nor was she certain why she felt this sudden compelling need to visit the cemetery where her ancestors and their bizarre and incestuous secrets were buried.

Locals called New Orleans graveyards the Cities of the Dead and from the little Jacinth had seen of them, the rows of sun-bleached crypts did resemble a city bereft of life.

Jacinth had only been inside the cemetery that housed the crumbling Villaré tomb once. She hadn't expected the visit to disturb her, but the second she'd stepped inside the rusty iron gate, the presence of death had become frigid, bony fingers clutching at her soul.

Ghostly shadows had stalked her, and every crypt she'd passed had seemed to be calling to her, luring her into the depths of darkness. She'd claimed a sudden migraine and left before reaching the famed Villaré crypt with its life-size chipped Madonna and jagged winged angels.

Today, she wouldn't run from shadows or cower in fear of invisible ghosts. Not even the rain could stop her from visiting the graves of all the people whose names had been printed on the family tree.

Her father's family. Her link to the past. A link that would hopefully reveal why her mother had been so traumatized that she'd fled this city that Jacinth had already learned to love.

Jacinth needed answers, and she planned to get them. Starting today.

Not that she was foolish enough to traipse through the spooky cemetery alone. Muggers loved the narrow paths flanked by crypts, some taller than a giant, where they could lie in wait for unsuspecting tourists and their wallets.

Jacinth had called ahead and arranged for Caitlyn's

newly hired tour guide to accompany her. Jacinth had never met Harvey Burgess, but Caitlyn was pleased with him. She claimed that even the most aggressive of the muggers had learned not to mess with Harvey.

The rain was falling in sheets by the time Jacinth reached the cemetery. She waited in her car as she kept an eye out for the guide. When he hadn't shown in fifteen minutes, she called him.

"I'm here," she said, once they'd moved past the greetings. "Parked just across the street from the front gate."

"You're kidding, right?"

"No. When we talked, you said you'd meet me here at one."

"When we talked, there was only a light mist falling. Now there's a monsoon. I assumed you'd cancel your plans."

"I figure the rain will let up any minute now."

"Not according to the radar. We're in the middle of a cluster of thunderstorms. How about postponing this until Wednesday? Or you can tag along on one of my regular tours on Monday or Tuesday."

"I'll be teaching or in class every afternoon and evening this week. This really is my only opportunity."

"I'm sorry, Jacinth, but even if the rain stops now, you could trip just maneuvering down those rocky, uneven paths. Believe me, even the muggers won't be out there today. Call me next weekend. We'll see if we can set something up."

"Thanks." To say she was disappointed would be a major understatement.

"Have you heard from Caitlyn?" Harvey asked.

"She called this weekend. The honeymoon is going well."

"Glad to hear that. Tell her not to have too much fun. We had so many tourists show up last night, I had to a turn down a few paying customers."

"I'll pass that on."

"Good. That will get her back on the job."

Reluctant to drive in the blinding rain, Jacinth decided to just stay put until there was a break in the storm. Her thoughts returned to the new information she'd discovered within the Villaré family Bible.

Marie had given birth to two children. Tabatha had choked to death at the age of three months, four years before Micah was conceived. There was no mention at all of a stepson or of anyone named Luther.

Marie's parents were Elizabeth and Jonathan. They had four sons in rapid succession. Ten years later, Marie came along.

And then there was the real shocker, the fact that had seared itself into Jacinth's brain.

Marie and Nathanial Villaré were siblings, though Nat was twelve years her senior.

Jacinth's father must have known his parents were brother and sister, but had he shared that with his wife or had it been kept a dark, family secret? Had Sophie found out and become enraged that she hadn't been told before she married Micah and gave birth to Jacinth and Caitlyn? Was that why she'd left and never again acknowledged Marie's existence?

If that's how it went down, Jacinth could understand

her mother's anger. Jacinth and her sister were perfectly healthy, but when they were younger, their mother must have lived in fear that they'd suffer from a genetic disorder caused by Marie's incestuous conception.

And what effect if any would that have on Jacinth's children? Or Caitlyn's? She'd definitely have to consult a geneticist for advice.

Eventually, the worst of the thunderstorm blew over and the rain slowed to a drizzle, though clouds still hovered threateningly and thunder rolled in the distance. The break in the storm was what she'd counted on when she'd driven to the cemetery in the rain.

The paths through the cemetery were no doubt as slick and treacherous as Harvey had said, but Jacinth had come prepared. She'd worn the rubber-sole tennis shoes with slip-resistant traction that she'd bought last summer for hiking in the Appalachian foothills.

All she needed now was Harvey.

But not to protect her from thugs. The cemetery was mugger-free, guaranteed. Plus, she'd already psyched herself up to walk through this particular City of the Dead and view the burial crypts of the famed and infamous Villarés.

It was the only way she could ascertain that the names of the buried matched the names in the Bible. A test to make sure the disturbing written record wasn't some kind of twisted family prank.

If she hurried she could do that and be back to the car before the next showers started. If not, getting wet wouldn't kill her. She had everything to gain and nothing to lose.

Leaving her purse in the trunk and out of sight where she'd tossed it for safekeeping before leaving home, Jacinth got out of the car, locked it and strode toward the intimidating gate. The ghostly squeak as she pushed it open brought gooseflesh to her arms and sent chills up the back of her neck.

But this wouldn't take long, she assured herself. Caitlyn had explained the exact location of the elaborate tomb on the first day she'd visited it and then again on the day Jacinth had faked the migraine.

Take the first sharp left, the first sharp right, and then follow a short meandering path toward the largest tree in the lot. The path literally dead-ended at the cross-shaped crypt.

If she walked really fast, she could get there, check it out and be back at her car in under fifteen minutes.

She started walking, head down to avoid stamping through the deepest of the puddles. "I'm not afraid," she said. "Do you hear me?" She was almost shouting now, the echo of her own voice somehow reassuring. "I'm not the least bit nervous about walking among the dead."

Something fell from a top branch, landing on the walk just in front of her. Spooked, she jumped off the path and her right foot sank into the muddy earth.

Just a harmless pinecone, Jacinth. Stop reacting like a kid in a Halloween haunted house.

She took deep breaths as she made the first sharp turn and tried to focus on the intricately carved symbols, angels and spires stretching into the foggy mist.

She made the left turn and then stopped, holding her

breath as a new sound played havoc with her resolve. There it went again and this time there was no mistaking the squish of footsteps on soggy ground somewhere off to her left. But all she could see were the carved angels and trumpets and ornate crosses reaching toward the sky.

Panic hit fast and hard. Muggers or ghosts, she didn't know or care. She was getting out of here. Now!

She took off running. Water splashed onto her legs. The wind tore off her only rain hat and sent it sailing to the top of an angel's harp. Jagged rocks reached out to try and trip her. Still, she kept running. The gate had to be close.

Only it wasn't.

Lungs burning and legs aching, Jacinth slowed to try to get her bearings.

"Wait!"

The call was almost swallowed by a violent clap of thunder. Jacinth glanced over her shoulder. Big mistake. A jagged piece of rock from the uneven stone walkway caught her toe and sent her sprawling facedown into the mud.

Before she could get up, two strong hands reached out to her and pulled her to her feet.

"Didn't anyone ever tell you to stay out of the rain?"

"NICK. WHAT ARE YOU doing here?"

"Performing my daily rescue. But you could make this a lot easier on me by staying inside in weather like this."

He pulled some clean dry tissues from his jacket

pocket and started wiping splatters of mud from her chin and mouth.

"Ouch."

"You've got a nasty scratch on your chin. I've got a first-aid kit in my truck."

"Forget the scratch. Back to my original question, what are you doing here?"

"Does that mean you're not glad to see me?"

"I'm thrilled that you're not a mugger—or worse. You didn't answer my question. Did you follow me?"

"Yeah," he admitted. "When I saw you drive off in the rain, I had a hunch you were up to something that could be dangerous."

"I would have been fine if you hadn't frightened me."

"Unless I'd actually been a mugger." Or worse. Like the man who'd decapitated their unidentified victim. He didn't even want to go there.

"I had it on good authority that muggers stay inside in this kind of weather."

"Because they don't expect to find anyone to mug. So why did you pick today to visit a cemetery?"

"I found an old Bible this morning, complete with a family tree that dates back to pre–Civil War days."

"And the Bible told you to visit a cemetery?"

"Of course not. I discovered some disconcerting things and I just wanted some backup endorsement of their validity."

So she'd come here alone without even a phone call to him. She didn't owe him explanations for what she did or where she went, but he felt strangely betrayed all the same. Odd coming from him when the whole reason they'd met had been due to his ulterior motives.

"Want to share what you learned?"

She nodded and shoved her windblown hair behind her ears.

Even with wet hair, she was gorgeous. He reached into his pocket, pulled out her scrunched-up rain hat and handed it to her. "You might need this before the tour is over."

"Thanks." She plopped it on her head and pushed her long hair inside it. She looked around. "Do you know where we are in relation to the Villaré family crypt?"

"It's right in front of you."

She bit her bottom lip as she stared at the impressive structure. "I was running in the wrong direction all the time."

"It's easy to get turned around in here." Fortunately, she didn't question how he knew exactly where to find the elaborately decorated tomb with its six-feet-tall angels looking over the ornately carved praying Madonna.

"It's magnificent," she murmured. "The artwork is exquisite." She walked over and rested her hands on the four-foot-tall black iron fence that surrounded the family tomb. "Is the fence to keep people out?"

"It isn't tall enough for that. It's mostly decorative but I suppose it keeps gawking tourists from trampling the grass growing around the tomb."

"What a remarkable tribute to the dead."

"New Orleans is known for its respect for the dead, but the tombs aren't just for show."

"I know. Caitlyn explained the problems caused by the high water table in this area. She said coffins buried in the ground can literally float away."

"And they sometimes do, especially after a big rain."

"I'd love to look inside the crypt."

"I doubt it's locked."

Nick lifted the latch and held the gate open while she entered. He did the same with the arched wooden door that opened into the tomb itself.

This time he entered first, clearing cobwebs with a brush of his hand. The air inside was musty and rank, not from the bodies but from the climate and lack of fresh air.

Jacinth hesitated at the door. Nick reached behind him and took her hand. It was icy-cold. "You're not afraid of being in a crypt, are you?"

"It's just so dark."

"C'mon in. Your pupils will adjust. Hang on to me until they do and you'll be fine."

She stepped inside cautiously. He reached into his jacket pocket with his free hand, the one Jacinth wasn't clutching so tightly he could barely wiggle his fingers. Fortunately the flashlight he'd dropped into it hadn't bounced out when he'd had to run to keep up with Jacinth.

He sprayed light over the vaults in the wall where the coffins were stored and then on an impressive plaque and a list of names inscribed on a large tombstone near the back of the tomb.

Jacinth let go of his hand and advanced for a better look. "'Victoria Villaré, 1845 to 1906,'" she read aloud from the plaque. "'Her brave actions saved the lives of countless Confederate soldiers. Admired by all. Loved by her family. Welcomed home by God.'"

"Quite a woman," Nick said. "No wonder her life-size portrait commands the spot on the landing."

"And it helps explain my grandmother's leaving the Villaré house to Caitlyn and me, when she'd been shut out of our lives for so long. I think it was her way of insuring that the Villaré legacy stayed in the family."

"And why she lived with her relics."

Jacinth grew quiet as she studied the list of the dead. When she found Micah's name, she traced the letters with her fingertips. Then one fingertip went to her eye to trap an escaping tear.

"Micah Villaré," she said. "Rest in peace. I know I would have loved you, Dad, had I been given the chance. Mom loved you so very, very much."

Nick tensed at the last part of the statement. Jacinth had her reality. He had his. The differences were a gap that couldn't be bridged. In case Nick needed a reminder, this was it.

"It's so sad that my father's life was stolen before Caitlyn and I could even get to know him. I'm glad the man who murdered him was sentenced to life in prison."

Nick's muscles tensed and he killed the beam from the flashlight, plunging them into the gray gloom of the crypt's interior. "Conviction doesn't necessarily mean guilt."

"What's that supposed to mean?"

He fought to tamp down his sudden anger and keep his words from coming out as husky growls. "Exactly what I said. Juries aren't some unfailing entity sent from God. They're human. They make mistakes, just like the rest of us. There are plenty of innocent people in prison."

Jacinth stared at him as if he'd sprouted an extra eye in the middle of his forehead. Sweat trickled down the back of his neck. The musty air clogged his lungs.

He moved toward the open door. "Are you ready to go?"

Jacinth's hands flew to her hips. "No. I haven't even finished reading the names. But you can go," she said. "I can find my way back to my car."

Now he'd set her off. Definitely not his intention. He turned on the flashlight and handed it to her. "Take all the time you need."

"Thanks. If I hit an exposed nerve, I'm sorry, Nick."

"Don't give it another thought." He did enough of that for both of them.

Nick stepped to the door and assumed the post of sentinel. Just in case there was a mugger out and about today, this crypt would be a bad place to get cornered. He'd hate to have to shoot some lout looking for money to buy his next fix.

"Victoria Villaré was not only heroic, she was the first one buried here," Jacinth announced. "This must have been built in her honor. But there are over fifteen names here. Does that mean that every one of the fifteen—except my father whose body was never found—were buried inside this one tomb?"

"That's usually what it means."

"Surely, there's not room for that many coffins in the wall vaults."

"Probably not, but families can choose to incorporate a kind of revolving coffin system. Dump the old, make way for the new—or rather the newly dead."

"Is that legal?"

"It's fully approved and not as callous as it sounds. The dead have never complained."

"Still, poor Victoria. It's her tomb and she was probably evicted years ago."

"Victoria's fame may have exempted her from the rotation."

"Is there some kind of order to who gets expelled from the vaults?"

"More or less. When someone new dies, they normally move the oldest bones to a fancy body bag and fit that into the back or sides of the vault. The old coffin is destroyed and the coffin holding the newest addition replaces it."

"I guess that makes sense when you think about it. According to the dates on the family tombstone, Marie is the latest addition and the only one added since my father. There's no one named Luther."

"There's no law that says you have to be buried with your ancestors."

"I know, but Luther's name wasn't in the Bible, either. And there were no other spouses listed for Nathanial or Marie so I don't see how he could be a stepson."

Nick had to watch what he said here. Say too much and he'd blow his cover before he was ready. Or he could just come out with the truth and destroy his best chance of clearing his father's name before the cancer he was fighting delivered an early death sentence.

"What else did you learn from the family tree?" he asked, changing the subject.

"That Marie had a daughter several years before she gave birth to my father. Tabatha Ruth. She only lived a few months. Her name is on the crypt tombstone, too. Hers must have been a tiny coffin."

A booming clap of thunder and a gust of cold wind pushed some much needed fresh air into the tomb. "Sounds as if the next howling thunderstorm is about to hit," Nick said.

"We should go." Jacinth trailed her fingers over her father's name one last time and then briefly bowed her head. Nick stepped outside to wait.

"There is one more thing," she said as she joined him. "It's the real reason I felt compelled to come to the cemetery today."

Now they were getting somewhere. "What is it?"

"Marie and Nathanial Villaré were not only man and wife, they were brother and sister, both having the same mother and father."

That was news. Odd that this fact had remained secret through a long and drawn-out murder trial. But then Nick was convinced that a lot of facts had been swept under the rug. Like evidence that had allowed the real killer to go free.

A bolt of lightning struck much too close, the electricity shooting a straight path from sky to ground.

"We'd best make a run for it," Jacinth said, her gaze fixed on the darkening sky.

"Let's stick with a fast walk. I don't want to spend the rest of the day doctoring your scratches."

She punched him in the arm and took off, striding at a pace almost equal to his normal jog. He hurried to catch up with her as the rain began to pelt them. By the time they reached the front gate, they were both drenched.

"Your car's closer," Nick said. "Why don't I drive it home and come back for my truck later, when the deluge has passed?"

"Deal. I don't drive well in monsoons."

She handed him the key just before they jumped the curb-high river and sprinted across the street.

"That will teach you to sneak around and follow me," she said, once they were inside the dry car.

He started to respond, quip for quip, but when he turned to face her, the words flew right out of his mind. She'd yanked off the rain hat. Water dripped from her dark hair and the tip of her perfect nose. In spite of all she'd been through the past two days, her dark eyes still sparkled. Her teasing smile wrapped around him like an open fire on a frigid night.

He'd told the truth about one thing. He didn't want to spend the afternoon smearing her with antiseptic. He wanted to spend it in her arms, making love.

He leaned over, slipped his arm around her and kissed her. Wet, wild, wonton. Forbidden fruit for all the right and wrong reasons.

He'd never wanted a woman more.

THIS KISS TOOK JACINTH by complete surprise. Her body reacted with a slow burn that crept deep inside her.

Forgetting everything but the here and now, she gave in to her ravenous hunger for Nick.

He cradled her head in his hand, his fingers tangling in her wet hair while his tongue explored the crevices of her mouth. When he finally pulled away, her kiss-swollen lips ached for more.

She took a deep breath and tried to make sense of her all-consuming desire for a man she barely knew.

Nick started the engine and switched the air controls to defrost.

"What brought that on?" she asked, genuinely puzzled.

"The fog on the windows or the kiss?"

"The kiss. I could have sworn you were irritated with me back at the crypt. You seemed distant at best and then all of a sudden you're acting as if you're starving and I'm dinner."

"I have this thing about women who look like drowned rats," he teased. "Guess I should have warned you."

"No joking your way around the subject this time, Nick. You go to all the trouble to follow me in the rain, supposedly to offer protection, which you do. Then you deliberately try to annoy me with uncalled-for comments about my father's killer."

"You were the one who got irritated. I was just stating facts."

"Unnecessary, exasperating facts that were obviously meant to annoy me. And then the next thing I know you're kissing me senseless."

"The kiss wasn't planned."

"I'm not complaining, and I'm certainly not looking for any level of commitment. I just want to know what's going on. Are you genuinely attracted to me or playing some stupid game where only you know the rules?"

"Jacinth, there's not a man alive who wouldn't find you attractive."

"That's a cop-out, not an answer."

"Okay. In case you actually can't tell from that kiss, I'm attracted to you. More than attracted. But you've got a lot on your plate right now. Falling body parts. A police investigation. A mysterious past you're trying to get a handle on. In my book, that makes you exceedingly vulnerable, and I don't like the idea of taking advantage of you."

He'd been honest. She owed him the same in return. She rested a hand on his thigh and felt his muscles tighten beneath his jeans.

"For the record, Nick, I'm extremely attracted to you, as well. But feeling this strongly about someone I've just met is completely out of character for me. Frankly, it scares the living daylights out of me."

"So we agree to go slow?"

"Agreed," she said.

But they both knew the promise was only words. Even now she felt desire burning hot inside her and she knew they'd make love. It was just a matter of time.

"Now that we've got passion and the possibility of hot sex out of the way, how about lunch?" Nick asked, reverting to teasing the way he always did when the conversation got sticky.

"Great. I'm starved," she agreed, "but I don't relish the idea of getting drenched again."

"We won't have to. I know this funky drive-through sandwich shop that has some of the best oyster po' boys in town. Tell me you eat oysters, Yankee-bred girl."

"As long as they're not raw. I don't like things sliding unaided down my throat."

"We'll work on that."

In less than five minutes, they were sitting at the microphone ordering their late lunch. She had hers dressed, a term she'd never heard used for sandwiches before she'd arrived in the Crescent City. It only meant the sandwich came with lettuce, tomatoes, onions and mayonnaise. Lots of mayonnaise. New Orleaneans liked their mayonnaise almost as much as they liked their Tabasco sauce.

When they were handed their order, Nick pulled into a parking space. It was still raining, but not as fiercely as it had been when they'd raced from the cemetery.

True to Nick's word, the po' boys were perfection. Wiping her mouth after every juicy bite, she managed to lose only one crispy oyster from between the crusty slices of French bread.

It fell to the seat between them. Nick rescued the fried morsel before she could pick it up and drop it into the empty bag.

"Twenty-second rule," he said, tossing it into his mouth.

"There's no such rule."

"Sure there is." He dabbed a dot of mayo from his lips. "As long as you pick it up in twenty seconds, it's still germ-free. And that oyster was too good to waste."

The rain slowed and finally stopped. Nick lowered the window, letting in some fresh air as he chewed his last bite. Jacinth had just started on her second half, but she was already getting full.

"When do you think we'll know something about Carrie?" she asked.

"I can tell you a little about her now."

He spouted information as if it were a memorized sales pitch. She was amazed at how much he'd learned in one morning. "You didn't mention an address."

He supplied that, as well.

"I have a student who lives in Westwego," she said. "Where is that exactly in relation to where we are now?"

"Across the Crescent City Connection, but less than an hour from here with just Sunday traffic to contend with."

She glanced at her watch—3:44. Not nearly as late as she'd thought. They could drop Nick off at his truck now that it wasn't pouring, drive home, shower and dress and still make it Carrie's house by seven at the latest.

It was a lot to squeeze into one day and it would leave Jacinth with little time to prepare for her morning class. But if she didn't go tonight, it might be days before she could get there.

So all she had to do was talk her protective private detective into a Sunday night road trip—one that wouldn't end with kisses. Unless…

CARRIE SAW THE LIGHTS of the pickup truck when it pulled into her driveway. Probably some lost fool turning around. She wasn't expecting company.

Only the truck didn't leave.

She walked to the window and pushed the blinds aside for a better look. A string of curses flitted through her mind as she watched Jacinth Villaré step out of the truck in her nice black slacks and soft purple sweater. Her thick, dark hair fell past her shoulders.

Impulsively, Carrie raked her fingers through her hair and jerked her tight yellow T-shirt down over her exposed abdomen. She might not be as classy and as pretty as Jacinth, but even at her age she still looked good.

Carrie didn't recognize the man with Jacinth, but he had a cop swagger and he reeked of authority. *Bring it on, copper. You got nothing on me.*

Oops. He could have if she wasn't careful. She dashed to her bedroom as the doorbell announced their arrival, grabbed her meager stash of marijuana and slid it between her mattress and box spring.

Then she sauntered back to the living room, flicked off the TV and smiled sweetly as she opened the door. She should make a stab at being gracious. After all, she and Jacinth Villaré were practically kin.

Chapter Six

Nick regretted his change of heart in bringing Jacinth along the minute he stepped through Carrie Marks's door. The scent of marijuana hung in the air along with a stench that suggested the kitchen garbage hadn't been carried out for days.

His gut feeling was that Carrie Marks was bad news and most of the time his first instincts were right on target.

Tonight he was to be Nick, friendly neighbor, with no mention of his last name. Better Carrie Marks didn't know he was a private detective. If she bothered to check, though, "Nick Bruno, Private Detective" was listed right there in her yellow pages. Right now, he wasn't even getting a notice.

"I've been dying to meet you, Jacinth," Carrie gushed. "I've started to drop by and introduce myself at least a dozen times."

"You should have," Jacinth said. "But better to call first. I work unpredictable hours."

"Not me, I'm same old, same old, day after day. Start

at dawn, but finish early. School cafeteria hours. I go to bed at nine most nights."

"We won't keep you long, but I'd really appreciate it if we could talk for a few minutes. I understand you knew my grandmother fairly well and she's a total mystery to me."

"You drove all the way out here on Sunday night to talk about Marie?"

"Her and Luther," Jacinth added. "I had no idea until yesterday that my father had a half brother."

"Wow. You have been kept in the dark. How did you hear about me or Luther?"

"From my neighbor, Gladys Findley. She mentioned how you had been a friend to Marie right up until she died."

"I did what I could since she didn't have family around. Luther always wondered why your mother snubbed the entire Villaré family after her husband was murdered."

"I'm sure she had her reasons for what she did," Jacinth said, her tone instantly defensive.

"You know her better than me," Carrie said with a shrug. "Come on in and have a seat. Just toss those magazines to the floor."

Nick picked up the magazines, noting titles as he did. Two copies of *Sports Illustrated*, one copy of a motorbike magazine, one on NASCAR racing and a couple of celeb fanzines.

Carrie grabbed a half-eaten bag of chips, a carton of dip and a couple of beer cans from the coffee table. "Let me clear this out of the way and I'll be right back."

"Take your time," Nick said.

"Can I get you two a beer or something?"

They both declined. Nick motioned Jacinth to the space he'd just cleared on the sofa and then scooted in beside her.

"She's friendly," Jacinth whispered.

With a figure she didn't get from beer, chips and dip. Someone was either still here or had just left. Likely a guy, judging from the reading material.

"Don't forget that we're here to ask questions, not answer them," Nick whispered.

"You mean like my talking about my mother?"

"Right."

"Got it."

Carrie rejoined them, settling into a chair with the same mustard-colored tweed upholstery as the couch. "How do you like living in the dilapidated morgue, as Luther used to refer to it?"

"Why would he say that?"

"He complained that all those portraits of deceased Villarés on the wall made the place seem like a shrine to the dead. He was always teasing Marie about her dedication to preserving history."

"The only portrait on the wall now is the life-size one of Victoria Villaré that hangs at the top of the landing," Jacinth said.

"Then someone must have taken them down after Marie moved into the nursing home. She would have never let them be moved while she was there to stop it."

"Do you have any idea who might have taken them?" Nick asked.

"Probably one of the greedy lawyers who probated Marie's estate," Carrie said angrily.

"Why take someone else's relatives home with you?"

"Marie made it a point to tell everybody that three of the portraits were museum quality, painted by a famous French artist back when the family still had money."

"I'd love to see those portraits," Jacinth said.

"You wouldn't be impressed. The heads were too big and looked like they were stuck on statues. I told Marie after Luther died that she should sell them and all that antique furniture and move in one of those fancy retirement homes where they cook all your meals for you. She wouldn't hear of it. She cared more about all those antiques than she cared about herself."

"The house was her legacy," Jacinth said.

"If the paintings were valuable works of art, they must have been insured," Nick said. He made a mental note to check into that later.

"You never know," Carrie said with a shrug. "They might have been worthless. Luther claimed his stepmother had delusions of past grandeur. You know, like the Villarés were royalty or something.

"She was a good person, though," Carrie added quickly. "When Luther told her we were getting married, she gave me a beautiful silver filigreed brooch with a sapphire-colored stone to welcome me into the family. She said it was a family heirloom."

"I'd love to see it," Jacinth said.

"I don't have it anymore. It was pretty but not my style. Luther took it to the pawnshop and got me fifty dollars for it."

"It's the thought that counts."

"That's what I said to Luther. Marie could be generous when she wanted to be. You know, now that I think about it, when Marie realized she was dying, she probably gave away those portraits."

That would have been an abrupt change of conviction, considering Carrie had just said Marie would never part with the paintings.

"So what do you want to know about Marie?" Carrie asked, obviously ready to drop the missing portraits speculation.

"Anything that would help me gain a better understanding of her. Her likes, dislikes, personality traits. Whatever stands out in your mind when you think of her."

Carrie curled her bare feet into the chair under her. "When I first met Marie, she reminded me of a queen living in her castle. She even dressed for dinner. And I never saw her without her hair styled and her makeup on."

"Did she have friends over?"

"I suppose, but she never talked about them to me. She was very cold and formal with me when we first met. I had the feeling she thought I wasn't good enough to marry her stepson."

"Wasn't Luther a lot older than you?" Nick asked.

"He was in his fifties. I was forty. That's not much difference these days."

"But Marie must have warmed up to you after she gave you the brooch."

"Not so much. She didn't get real friendly until

Luther disappeared while on that hunting trip in Alaska. Then Marie and I were both so scared, we clung to each other like we were all either of us had left in the world."

"Did the Alaskan police ever arrest a suspect?" Nick asked, though he knew from his own investigation that they hadn't.

"No. I'm not sure they tried very hard. All they ever found of Luther's were his gun and his wallet. They didn't find that until the spring thaw set in."

"Then what made them think he'd been murdered?" Jacinth asked.

"All the money was gone from his wallet. His watch was gone, too. His father had given him that before he died. Luther didn't go anywhere without that watch. It showed up later at a pawnshop in Juneau. And we would have heard from him had he still been alive."

"Marie must have been devastated," Jacinth said. "To lose a son and a stepson and never recover the body of either of them."

"She was. I tried to be there for her as often as I could after that, but she didn't want to do much but stay in that house and take care of her cat."

"I never knew," Jacinth said. "I never called, not even after Mother died. There's no excuse for that."

"Marie must have forgiven you," Carrie said. "She left you and your sister the house since Luther wasn't alive to inherit it. In the end, that house was the only thing she cared about, the only thing she had that was worth much."

"Except for the missing paintings," Nick interjected. "What do you know about Luther's real mother?"

Jacinth asked. "I couldn't find any record that Nathanial was ever married to anyone except Marie."

"That's because Nat never married Luther's mother. They met the year Nat studied in Italy. She worked in a tavern near the college. They were first loves. Luther was proud of that. Made him feel important even if he was illegitimate."

"What happened to break them up?"

"His mother had some rare form of blood disorder. She died right after Luther was born, but his dad told him about it. Nat came home and married Marie, so she could take care of the baby."

"That couldn't be right." Jacinth uncrossed her legs and leaned in closer. "Marie was twelve years younger than her husband. If Nat was just out of college, Marie would have only been about ten years old when Luther was born."

Carrie squirmed. "Right. I—I didn't mean he came home right then," she stammered. "He stayed in Italy for like a long time. But then he came home and married Marie when she was older."

Give a liar enough rope and time, and they'd always hang themselves. Nick had gotten what he came for. Proof that the majority of the Villarés were as self-serving as he'd believed. And anything Carrie Marks said was suspect.

"We should be going," he said.

"Yes," Jacinth agreed. "We've taken up enough of your time, Carrie. But I really appreciate your talking to me. I feel I know my grandmother and my dad's stepbrother a bit better now."

Carrie got out of the chair to see them out. "I hope I

didn't give you the wrong idea about Marie. She wasn't always the loner she was in the end. Luther said she had a lover for years, a man fifteen years younger than she was. No one seemed to know why they broke up. It was several years before I started dating Luther."

Nick's interest piqued. "Do you know the lover's name?"

"Sure. It was Eric Ladeaux."

"The name sounds familiar."

"He owns Swishers. You've probably never heard of it, Jacinth, but it's a Gentleman's Club in the Quarter."

Jacinth smiled. "So the Villaré queen had her wild side. Good for her."

Carrie opened the door. "Maybe we can have lunch together sometimes, Jacinth. I'd like for us to be friends. I think Luther and Marie would have liked that, too."

Nick wouldn't. He didn't trust Carrie Marks.

Everybody had a motive. Only Jacinth's was straight-forward and out in the open.

Which was why he couldn't go through with the plans he'd had when he moved next door to her. He couldn't use her, not even to free his father. He'd clear out of her life completely just as soon as he was certain she was safe from the killer who'd left body parts in the walls of her house.

He'd walk away on his own, before she discovered the truth about him and kicked him out.

JACINTH SWUNG HER BRIEFCASE and handbag straps over her shoulder, grabbed her laptop computer and did a final check of her hair and makeup in the mirror.

Satisfied that she looked the role of serious academia professional, she walked into the hall and called good-bye to Sin. The feline was busy performing her daily grooming tasks and ignored Jacinth, as always.

"Okay, Sin, you've made your point. I'm only important when I'm operating the can opener."

Jacinth hurried to the staircase. Her ride wasn't due to arrive for another fifteen minutes, but Dr. Reginald Jefferies was frequently early. He was her favorite professor—brilliant, super helpful, nice-looking in a tweedy sort of way.

His biggest drawback was that he tended to become so buried in the past he lost contact with the current century.

The portrait of the elegant Victoria Villaré with her condescending stare and stern expression caught Jacinth's attention as she reached the landing. She paused as last night's conversation came back to haunt her.

"So, lovely matriarch of the Villaré burial chamber, what happened to your relatives? And why did you get left behind, or were the marauders afraid to tear you from your place of honor?"

Too bad the image in the portrait couldn't talk. Imagine all the things she'd seen in this house since the 1860s. She'd know of flirtations and indiscretions and of how Marie decided that she'd marry her brother and raise his motherless child.

Had she been coerced into it by her parents, or perhaps feared becoming a lonely spinster? Or had she just loved Nat so much that she ignored customs and taboos?

The image staring back at her with the enchanting steel-gray eyes would also know who had buried a human head inside the bathroom's walls.

There was no way Victoria would talk, but Carrie Marks had certainly had plenty to say. Nick had cautioned Jacinth on the way home last night not to put a lot of faith in Carrie's observations and opinions, but Jacinth could think of no reason for her to lie.

Jacinth stepped onto the wide veranda and marveled at the beautiful, sunny calm that had followed yesterday's violent storms. Brisk air, a slight breeze and not a cloud in the brilliant blue sky.

The morning was only a few degrees short of perfection. Drop Nick into it and they'd be there.

A car pulled up in her driveway, but not the one she was expecting. Detective Greene opened the door of his unmarked black sedan and slid from behind the wheel. She walked out to meet him.

"Good to see you again but bad timing," she said. "My ride should be here any minute and I'll have to leave or cause us both to be late for work."

"This will only take a minute. Just stopped by to let you know we have an ID on the victim."

"Who was she?"

Jacinth spun around at the sound of Nick's voice. He was standing at the edge of her lawn, shirtless in spite of the slight chill in the air and wearing a pair of deep purple LSU running shorts that revealed lots of muscular thigh. Her knees went weak as desire hummed through her.

She took a deep breath and struggled to get the untimely explosion of sensual craving under control.

"Hi, Nick. Come over and I'll introduce you to Detective Greene."

"We've met," Ron said, "last year when Nick managed to destroy my open-and-shut rape case."

"You had the wrong man," Nick said. "But got to hand it to you. You ended up with the right thug behind bars. So who's the victim?"

"I guess I can tell you, too, since the local media already have the information."

"I trust you had the good sense not to make Jacinth's name and address public?"

"None of the pertinent details surrounding the case have been released—except the victim's name and fact that she was murdered. We'd like it to remain that way, so if you two will keep this under your hats until we have a suspect in custody, the department would appreciate it. We don't want some idiot copycat getting ideas."

"I haven't told a soul," Jacinth said. "And I won't."

"Good."

"The woman's name?" Nick asked again.

"Joy Adams."

"The prostitute who went missing last October?"

"You have a good memory," Greene said. "Did you know the woman?"

"Just know of her."

Professor Jefferies pulled up to the curb in a late-model Acura. "That's my ride," Jacinth said. She glanced at her watch. "I have to go, but if there's anything else I should know, you can leave a message at my cell phone number."

"That works," Greene said. "But one quick question. Does this house have any secret passageways?"

"I don't think so. I've never seen one or been told about one. Why?"

"Just curious. I know secret walkways were built into some of the plantation-style houses built during that period."

The detective did not strike her as the kind of cop who asked idle questions. "Are you suggesting the house could have a passageway within the walls with more bodies or body parts entombed inside it?"

"I'm not suggesting anything. I'm just considering all possible scenarios."

She got a sick feeling in the pit of her stomach.

Both men told her not to worry as she walked away. Fat chance she could follow that advice.

She looked back at the house as Professor Jefferies pulled away from the curb. The Greek columns, the verandas, the wide, shuttered windows. It still looked the same as it had before this weekend, but it wasn't the same in her mind. Now it was the backdrop for a gruesome decapitation.

She wondered if it would ever feel like home again.

NICK'S HEAD WAS REELING from the latest piece of information. Still he watched as the driver of the Acura leaned over and opened the door for Jacinth.

Salt-and-pepper hair. Wearing a sports coat. Probably a smooth talker, too. A twinge of jealousy knotted in Nick's gut, though he knew he had no right to the emotion.

Greene rocked back on his heels. "You do realize that Jacinth Villaré is out of your league, don't you?"

Nick nodded. "So far out I can't even see the stadium lights from here."

"Keep an eye on her, though. I'm not sure what we're dealing with but it can't be good."

"I plan to."

"Then I'll see you around."

Nick did a few quick stretches and then started his jog through the French Quarter as his mind tangled with the facts he knew and those he didn't.

Three women between the ages of twenty-one and twenty-five had been reported as missing over a three-month period last fall. All of them had worked as exotic dancers in the French Quarter, each at a different club.

There was no indication that they knew each other or were involved in any cults or criminal activity. In none of the instances had the police discovered evidence of foul play—until now.

Joy Adams had been the oldest of the missing women. Cecelia Davis had been a year younger. Jewel Benet had been the youngest.

Jewel's father had hired Nick to investigate his daughter's disappearance. Nick had spent hours on top of hours on the case, followed every hint of a lead. He'd gotten nowhere.

There had been no substantiated sightings, no paper trail, no charges to her credit card, no stalkers, no reported threats or problems with abusive boyfriends or overzealous customers. It was as if Jewel just woke up one morning and vanished into thin air.

Nick had become more convinced by the day that Jewel had been murdered. Eventually, her father came to that same conclusion and decided to give up his search.

Nick had stayed on the case even after he no longer got paid. He hated that he'd failed Jewel and her family and it bugged the hell out of him that he'd never found the body or the murder weapon.

As far as he knew the NOPD had never officially linked the cases of the missing women. They would have to now. There would be no justification for assuming the other two missing women had just moved on to the next town, the next club, the next man.

Sordid images pushed their way into Nick's brain. Jewel Benet, only twenty-one, rebellious, but beautiful and deeply loved by her parents. Abducted and brutally murdered by a cold-blooded killer and buried inside the wall of the Villaré mansion.

It was only speculation for Jewel. It was now a sure thing for Joy Adams. He couldn't help but wonder if she'd ever worked for Swishers, and if it was possible that Eric Ladeaux was connected to Joy's murder.

It was a definite that the monster who'd committed the horrific crime had been inside the house that Jacinth was living in now.

He'd probably been confident the evidence of his crime was hidden away forever. But as soon as he read the morning paper or saw the news on TV, he'd know that at least one of his atrocities had been uncovered.

Would he dare risk a return to the scene of the crime to destroy any remaining evidence?

Nick's lungs began to burn. He stopped for breath and realized that he'd run twice as far as he'd meant to and in far less time than it would have normally taken. He'd pushed his body to the limits. Now it was time to push his training and skills to the limit to find the killer before Jacinth wound up his next victim.

He'd fight the devil himself if that's what it took to keep her safe. Too bad no one had done that for Joy Adams.

NICK FOLLOWED A GROUP of rowdy conventioneers into the dimly lit foyer of Swishers. A few still wore their bright red-and-white name tags. Most didn't.

Eighties music blared from a speaker and a scantily clad, bosomy employee greeted the men and promised them tables near the action. Nick worked his way around the group and went straight to the long bar to the right of the entrance.

The bartender nodded to him but kept squirting gin into a row of martini glasses. Evidently the noontime crowd was thirsty.

A waitress appeared for the drinks the second they were ready, and the bartender, who looked to be in his early thirties, walked over to Nick.

"Not much action out here. Sure you don't want Susie to find you a table in the main club area?"

Nick checked out the man's name tag. "Not here for action, Bruce. I'm here to see Eric Ladeaux. Let him know I'm here, will you?"

"I'm afraid I can't do that. Eric's in New York for his granddaughter's wedding. He won't be back in the club until Friday."

"Then maybe you can help. How long have you been bartending here?"

"Five years, but I'm not usually behind the bar. Bella, the goddess of bartender fun, called in sick today."

"Where are you usually?"

"Wherever I'm needed. I'm the manager. So how can I help you?"

"Did Joy Adams ever dance here?"

"Ah, you're a cop. Should have known when you settled at the bar instead of going for the action."

"Actually, I'm a private detective, but since you assumed I'm here officially, I take it you've heard about Joy's murder."

"Yeah. Bad news. But I'm afraid I can't help you. I didn't know Joy Adams and she's never worked here. And since you're not a cop, I don't want you bothering my dancers with this. They get shook up enough when one of their own has been murdered. Spooked dancers aren't good for business."

"I have it on good authority that Ms. Adams did work here for a while," Nick said. A white lie, unless you considered a hunch good authority.

"Better look for new informants. I anticipated that question coming up today, so I looked up Joy's name in the personnel files when I reached the club this morning. She's never drawn a paycheck from Swishers."

"Is that the story you want to stick with?"

"Look…"

"Nick. Nick Bruno."

"Okay. Look, Nick. I have a business to run, but that doesn't make me a badass. If I knew Joy Adams, I'd admit it. If I had any idea who'd murdered her, I'd have called the cops and turned the information over to them. Now I have to get back to work."

He motioned to the other end of the bar. "You can see I've got waitresses lining up for their orders."

Nick glanced at the two waitresses Bruce had pointed out. The shapely blonde looked familiar. She looked away when she saw him watching her.

Nick slid off the bench and went down the hallway in search of the men's room. When he came out, the blonde stepped from the recessed area that led to the ladies' restroom.

She cozied up next to him and slipped something in his front jeans pocket. Before he could tell her he wasn't interested in a private rendezvous, she disappeared into the ladies' room.

Nick walked to the door, glad to escape the earsplitting volume of the music even if the visit to Swishers was a total washout.

He turned onto Bourbon Street. A group of women poured out of a T-shirt shop, all of them sporting colorful Mardi Gras beads even though the official festival season wouldn't start for months.

A guy was crowding the sidewalk, blowing "When the Saints Go Marching In" on his horn, the instrument's case opened and filled with tips from appreciative tourists.

Nick reached into his pocket for a few coins to add

to the musician's booty. His fingertips brushed the note from the blonde. He pulled it out. The note was wrapped around a small metal key.

Meet me in one hour at this address. It's about Joy Adams.

The address that followed was just a couple of blocks away. It sounded like a trap to Nick. He hated walking into a trap.

But at least he'd go prepared. His Glock was a great equalizer.

Chapter Seven

The address was in the middle of the block. The entrance was next to an antique shop and through a locked metal gate that opened into a narrow courtyard.

He tried the key. It turned easily and the rusting gate squeaked open. Pigeons scattered as he stepped inside. Wind chimes tinkled from a second-floor balcony. A dragonfly darted past him and then landed on the arm of a wrought-iron bench.

At least nothing resembled trouble—yet.

He climbed the outdoor stairwell and looked for apartment 206. Two hanging planters overflowing with greenery served as a welcome.

He put his hand to the butt of his gun and rang the bell. The blonde answered right away. "I'm glad you came," she said. "I've been sick with worry ever since I heard the news. When I saw you in Swishers, I took that as a sign."

He scanned what he could see of the apartment, a living and dining space with a back window that opened onto a view of the street. "Are we alone?"

"Yes. I'd rather no one know I've talked to you."

Hence the note stuck in his pocket. "I'm surprised you even heard me mention Joy's name over the club's loud music."

"I didn't. I recognized you."

"Have we met?"

"Two years ago. My sister hired you to find out if my cheating, lying brother-in-law was hiding money from her when they were going through their divorce."

Now he knew why she looked familiar. "You're Delaney Michael's sister. We met at her attorney's office. I forget your name, though."

"Sarah Livingston."

"Good to see you again, Sarah."

"I only have a few minutes," she said. "This is my lunch break. Do you mind if I finish eating while we talk?"

"Not at all."

She went to the kitchen and retrieved a sandwich with one bite missing. She didn't bother to sit, so he kept standing, as well.

"How do you know Joy Adams?"

"We were roommates."

"Bruce just swore to me that she'd never worked at Swishers."

"She didn't. We got to know each other in karate classes. I was forever a novice but Joy earned her black belt. We hit it off and decided to rent this apartment."

"Were you living together when she disappeared?"

"Yes, and we had been for six months."

"So what is it you want to tell me about her?"

"I think I know who killed her."

Nick was cautiously excited. He'd been down dead-end roads that looked like highways before. "I'm listening."

"She was really into some guy right before she disappeared. He told her he was a prince from some Scandinavian country, but he couldn't tell her which one because he was in the States secretly."

This was sounding fishier by the second. Nick stood with his back to the wall, half expecting burly guys to rush out of the bedroom and jump him at any second. "Why did his being in the States have to be kept secret?"

"I don't remember exactly, something about his not going through state department channels because he wanted to see the United States like any other tourist."

"Did the prince have a name?"

"He told Joy to just call him John. His hair was obviously bleached and he didn't look like a Scandinavian to me. But he gave Joy lots of tacky jewelry and he kept telling her he wanted to marry her and take her back with him to live as royalty."

"Did Joy take him at his word?"

"Yes, but you'd have to know Joy to understand why she'd fall for such bunk. In spite of being hurt by every guy she'd ever fallen for, she always believed her prince would show up one day."

"Can you describe this prince?"

"He was taller than average. Bleached hair, like I said. I saw him once, briefly, but didn't get a good look at him. But I can tell you he didn't look all that princely walking down Bourbon Street and chugging down a beer."

"Have you told all this to the police?"

"I told them last year when Joy first went missing. They left and never got back to me. I could tell they just thought Joy ran off with the guy. To be honest, I would have thought that, too, except she didn't take his gifts that she'd believed were worth a fortune."

"Then she didn't leave a message or try to get in touch with you?"

"No, but if Joy were all right, she would have found a way to get in touch with me."

Sarah's eyes welled with tears and she wadded the rest of her sandwich into the napkin and tossed it into the trash. "Joy loved him and he killed her. He should pay, Nick. Someone should make him pay."

"Someone should—*if* he's the killer. We don't have proof of that yet. Do you still have the gifts he gave Joy?"

"I do. Wait here and I'll get them for you."

She returned a minute later with a plastic shoe box. She opened it and set it on the counter next to the sink. "*John* claimed these were heirlooms that had been in his family for generations."

"They do look old," Nick said.

"Actually, they look like the tacky stuff my grandmother wears, and, believe me, she's not royalty."

Nick leaned over for a better look. There were at least a dozen pieces of jewelry—necklaces, earrings, pins, bracelets. They ran the gamut of design, but all looked to be antique.

He reached into the shiny mix and picked up a gold bracelet with delicate heart-shaped links. It looked real enough to Nick, not that he was an expert in jewelry. He wore a plain, leather-band watch and had never owned a ring. He'd never bought one for anyone else, either.

He sifted to the bottom of the box and let his fingers come to rest on an ornate, silver filigreed brooch with a blue stone in its center. Probably at least similar to the one Marie Villaré had given Carrie when she thought she was going to become part of the family.

"Have you had the jewelry appraised?"

"Not these pieces, but I took in a couple of the rings that John had claimed were priceless. The jeweler said they were the kind of costume jewelry you can pick up at garage sales for ten or fifteen dollars. I wore them for a while, but threw them in the trash when they turned my fingers green.

"I kept these thinking Joy might come back for them. Now I know she never will." Sarah's eyes teared up again as she snapped the lid back on the box. "You can take the jewelry with you if you think it will help in finding her killer."

"Thanks." He slipped the brooch he was still holding into his pocket. "Unless we discover the jewelry is stolen property or evidence in a murder case, I'll get them back to you."

Nick's best hunch right now was that Prince John had stolen the jewels from Marie and used the baubles to lure at least three young women to their deaths. Now all he needed was to find this John when he didn't have a solid description or a last name.

Worse, he had no clue if the killer was connected to

Marie Villaré in some way or had just broken into the house while it was empty.

"I'll get out of here now and let you get back to work," Nick said, "but I may need to talk to you again."

"No problem. Just don't come around the club to talk."

"I guess Bruce frowns on your having personal conversations on company time."

"Bruce is fine. I'd just rather Eric Ladeaux not find out I'm talking to a private detective about Joy."

"Why would he care? You and Bruce both claimed there was no connection between Joy and Swishers."

"I said Joy didn't work for Swishers. I never said there was no connection between her and Eric."

If this kept up, Nick was going to need a scorecard to keep up with the suspects. "What was the connection between Joy and Ladeaux?"

"They were lovers. Joy broke it off with him when her prince came along."

The plot was thickening to mud. It would take hours to catch Jacinth up to speed on everything that he'd learned today.

He'd make one quick stop and drop the shoe box full of treasures off with a jeweler friend of his so that he could get a true appraisal. And then it was back to the Villaré mansion and Jacinth. He planned to be there waiting when she returned home.

He had to tell her the full truth about the three women who'd disappeared, had to admit that the beast who'd killed Joy Adams might well have killed all three of them and perhaps others.

And then he'd lay down the rules for keeping Jacinth safe. He was taking no chances with her life.

He'd just started down the stairs, shoe box in hand, when he felt the hammerlike blow to the back of his skull.

The world spun around him as he stumbled and careened down the steep steps to the concrete courtyard below. His vision blurred and then turned off like a lightbulb.

When he came to, his head hurt like hell. An elderly woman with a cane was standing over him, staring disgustingly as if he were rubbish that had missed the Dumpster.

The plastic shoe box was nowhere to be seen.

JACINTH MADE HER SECOND call of the afternoon to Nick. Again, there was no answer. Frustration made her edgy. It wasn't that she had news for him. She just needed to make contact. With all that was going on, he seemed her only link to sanity.

Not that she should expect him to be at her beck and call. He had his own cases to work on just as she had her responsibilities at the university.

Today had been nonstop. Arrangements for a guest lecturer and a meeting with her doctorate advisor had to be integrated with her already full teacher/grad student schedule. It was four-thirty now and she hadn't even managed to find time for lunch.

But at least the demanding workload had given her some reprieve from the horrors of the past weekend. Now that she had a moment to catch her breath, the problems and the murder were closing in again and she felt as if she were caught in a dangerous undertow that was pulling her beneath a torrent of gray, deadly waves.

Her nerves were frayed and there was no respite in sight. Her spirits plunged with her energy level. She was positively exhausted. The last three restless nights were taking their toll.

Her inexplicable infatuation with Nick wasn't helping.

He was complicated and frustrating, savior and tormentor at the same time.

He'd moved in fast, rushing to her rescue, voluntarily taking on a dirty plumbing job, following her to the cemetery just be certain she was safe—or so he'd claimed.

He was seemingly as infatuated with her as she was with him, yet he pulled away every time things between them started heating up. She'd be far less perturbed and more trusting of his motives if they made sense to her.

She looked up at a light tapping. Dr. Jefferies smiled from her doorway. "Do you want to grab a bite to eat before class?"

"Either that or a nap."

"You do look rather exhausted."

"Thanks. I needed that."

"Sorry, but you do. Doctoral studies paired with a teaching assistantship can sometimes become overwhelming. If you're having problems handling everything, you should speak to your advisor."

"It's not that. It's personal issues," she offered, unwilling to say more and pull him into her mire.

"We're all really pleased with your work, Jacinth. You're exactly the caliber of doctoral candidate we love to get. But if you need a few days' leave to take care of personal matters, that can always be arranged."

"Thanks. I'm good for now but I'll keep that in mind."

"Then will you join me in a quick bite before class?"

She nodded. "But we'll have to make it fast. The students in my evening classes like to start at straight up six o'clock so I dismiss them on time."

Tonight, she'd be more than ready to leave, herself.

They opted for a nearby coffee shop. Jacinth was in serious need of caffeine, but she chose mineral water with a bowl of vegetable soup. She was desperate for a good night's sleep tonight.

"I visited the Villaré family crypt yesterday," she said while they waited for their order.

Dr. Jefferies's eyebrows arched. "In those thunderstorms?"

"I admit I picked a poor day for the adventure. But the crypt was worth getting wet."

"Yes. It's been featured in several articles about New Orleans cemeteries."

"I didn't realize that, but I can see why. However, the visit was personal for me. My father's body was never found, but his name is carved into the large family tombstone."

"You'd seen it before, of course?"

"No. I've been busy with house repairs and renovations." She was not getting into her aversion to ghostly confines with Dr. Jefferies. "There was a plaque that mentioned Victoria Villaré's heroism during the Civil War."

"Ah, yes, Victoria the Brave. She was in her teens when key officers in the Union Army booted her family from the premises and seized the Villaré house for their own use. Victoria used the secret passageway's corridors to overhear the officers' strategies. Many saved lives were accredited to her."

"So the house I'm living in really does have a hidden passageway that would allow someone to come and go unnoticed?"

"Well, it did at one time. I suspect the passage was sealed off years ago."

"Why seal it off?"

He worried a small mole on his neck as if it were the key to his vast store of knowledge. "Rats. At one time, they became a real plague to the city. After a couple of people died from rodent bites, it was determined that many of the filthy rodents bred in the dank and useless passageways. At that point, home owners couldn't seal them off fast enough."

The man might not have a social life, but he was a walking encyclopedia. "How would I check to see if the passageway in my house had been sealed?"

"Locate the entrance."

"How would I do that? Is there some mark on the wall I should look for?"

"If they were easy to find, they wouldn't be called secret passageways, but rest easy, Jacinth. The Villarés were members of the socially elite back in those days.

I'm certain your passageway is sealed. No rats will invade your living space."

Dr. Jefferies's assurance was comforting.

But what if he was wrong?

"I'd love to know more about how the passageways were constructed and used."

"Then I have a good friend you should talk to. Her name is Eugenia Kibecti and she and her husband own a house on the historic registrar with a functioning secret passageway. I'm sure she'd be glad to give you a tour if you asked."

"I just may do that." Hopefully Eugenia's passageway did not contain body parts.

JACINTH WAS BEYOND exhaustion when she swung out of Dr. Jefferies's car at half-past nine and hurried up her walk.

"Long day."

Startled, she jumped, banging her shoulder against the nearest Greek column. "Nick. Don't you ever give warning before you pop up?"

"It's not like I'm hiding. I'm sitting in your porch swing."

She was glad to see him, but still irrationally irritated that he hadn't called. "Why are you sitting there? It's late."

"Educator's hours?"

The hint of sarcasm in his voice increased her frustration. "As a matter of fact, I teach a freshman research class twice a week that lets out at nine. I would have explained that had you answered my calls."

"I was out of commission for a while. Fortunately, your friend waited around to drive you home."

She leaned against the column. "Don't tell me you're jealous, Nick. Not after you lectured me on why our attraction for each other had to be locked away and forbidden to even rear its sensual head."

"Let's start over. We're both just a little undone tonight." Nick rose from the swing and walked over to her. "We need to talk."

One look at him in the glow of the porch light and her anxiety level soared. She gingerly touched a finger to his bruised and swollen face, then noticed the lump on the back of his head. "What happened?"

"I took an ugly fall, nothing serious. Don't worry. I've had the lump checked out. I'm fine."

"This has to do with Joy Adams, doesn't it?"

"It's a long story. I can talk better inside."

She unlocked the door, dreading what would come next.

Nick walked over to the porch swing and retrieved a small duffel she hadn't noticed before. "What's in there?"

"Important developments. I'll explain it."

"Before or after you tell me why you look like you fell into a tiger's cage?"

"It's all connected."

Her brain reeled from apprehension and the numbing fatigue that refused to let go of her.

"I need a minute to change into something more comfortable and splash some cold water on my face to jump-start my weary brain."

"Mind if I brew a pot of coffee while you do?"

"Go ahead, but none for me. The coffee's in a canister just above the pot. So are the filters."

Sin was waiting at the top of the stairs, but when Jacinth approached, she yowled and ran down the hall, disappearing into Marie's old bedroom.

Jacinth started to her own room, but paused when she caught a whiff of that same unpleasant odor she'd noticed when she returned from the store on Saturday. Only this time she knew exactly what it smelled like— the dank, moldy stench of mildew and stale air that she'd breathed inside the crypt.

She had to get the plumber out here to find that leak in the wall soon or she'd get sick from the mold.

Jacinth unzipped her straight black skirt and stepped out of it. While she unbuttoned her blouse, she opened the closet to retrieve her blue silk robe.

She jumped back, fright hitting so hard, she had to fight to hold back tears. Books and files that had been stored in heavy boxes on the top shelf of the closet were scattered all over the floor. Coats had been yanked from their hangers and left to tangle with the rest of the mess.

No way could she blame this mess on Sin.

Someone had broken into the house while she was at the university. But who? And why?

She backed away from the closet as terrifying possibilities haunted her mind. She should call Detective Greene. He should know about this.

When she reached for her phone, she noticed a small placard on her pillow, the words on it neatly printed in black. She dropped to the side of the bed and picked it up.

Thou shalt not steal.

The wages of sin is DEATH!

She dropped the note as if it were poison.

Joy Adams's killer had been in this very room today. There was no other explanation. Emotions raged inside her, shifting and changing so fast she didn't know what she was feeling.

Her fingers closed around the nearest relief valve, a thick volume of historical vignettes. She threw the book against the wall as hard as she could. Then, shaking so badly she could barely stand, she kicked out of her black pumps sending them flying across the room and dropped onto the bed.

She should have never come back to New Orleans.

Chapter Eight

Nick was reaching for a mug from the cabinet when he heard a loud clunk coming from somewhere above him, as if something—or someone—had been hurled against the wall. Two more thumps followed, not as loud at the first.

His adrenaline kicked into overdrive. He grabbed his Glock from his duffel and raced toward the staircase. His training clicked in like instinct, his mind going over a mental checklist of how not to give the enemy the advantage.

Once upstairs, he noticed everything at once, but followed the sound of a low wail he wasn't even sure was human that came from midway down the long hallway. He stopped just outside the open door to assess the situation.

He spotted Jacinth instantly. But no intruders. No spilled blood. No evidence of injury. No evidence of danger. Yet every muscle in his body grew rock hard as he faced the one situation his training hadn't addressed.

Jacinth was facedown on the bed, beating her fists into her pillow as if she were training for a boxing match. Her blouse was bunched up almost to her shoulder blades. Below the waist, she was wearing nothing but a black thong.

His mouth went dry, and blood rushed to his head with such force he grew dizzy. He fisted and unfisted his hands, trying to get control of his libido before he walked over to Jacinth and really put temptation to the test.

"What happened?" he managed, his tone husky with emotions he didn't want to feel.

She kicked her feet against the quilt like a two-year-old throwing a tantrum and then rolled over. When she saw him, her eyes flashed fire.

"We don't have to talk, Nick. You don't have to keep running over to protect me from a lunatic killer anymore. *I give up!*"

He placed his gun on her marble-topped dresser. "I'm not sure that's an option."

She threw her legs over the side of the bed. "I just made it one. I'm moving out. Tonight. And I'll call Caitlyn and tell her to just keep traveling with Marcus to all his photo shoots because Grandmother Villaré bequeathed us a killer's lair, not a home."

Nick scanned the room, still with no clue what had caused Jacinth's meltdown. "What just happened here? Did you get a phone call from someone?"

"Oh, way better than that. I got an anonymous note, personally delivered."

"Where is this note?"

She felt around on the bed until she located it beneath the pillow she'd been attacking. "It doesn't have my name on it, but I'm sure it was intended for me, sinner that I am." She handed him the now creased and wrinkled note.

Nick read and reread it. "The son of a bitch."

"I have worse names for him. He was here, Nick. In my bedroom while I was at work. Apparently he thinks this house he's made into a morgue is his."

"You have every reason to be upset, Jacinth."

"You think?"

"Yes, but you need to settle down so that we can reason this through."

"How do you reason with a madman?"

"We could stick to the facts. First, we don't know for certain that the man who killed Joy Adams is the same one who left the note."

"So there may be two murdering lunatics who come in and out of this house at will. That makes me feel so much better."

"I'm just trying to figure why Joy Adams's killer would insinuate that you stole something that was his."

"Maybe he worked for Marie. He could be a plumber, or a yard boy, or a window washer. It takes a village to keep this money pit from collapsing. There's a new catastrophe every day."

"Working for someone doesn't entitle you to their property."

"Well, he was definitely looking for something when he trashed my closet."

"Whoa. You lost me there. When did your closet get trashed?"

"Today, no doubt when the killer was delivering my love letter."

The confusion started to clear. Jacinth had gotten a double whammy when she came upstairs tonight, and he was about to hit her again.

She stood and jerked her blouse together as if she'd just realized her bra and the soft mounds of her breasts were exposed. "You want the house, Nick? You take it."

"How about I just move in with you?" That was not the way he'd rehearsed the offer. But she was thinking it over. He could see the deliberation in her eyes and the slight pucker of her brow.

"If you don't want me to stay here, then come and stay with me," he offered.

"Your apartment's barely big enough for you."

"I have a friend in Gretna with a house that's sitting empty. He'd let us stay there until Joy Adams's killer is behind bars. Or we can drive down the bayou to my fishing cabin. Your call."

"Why do you keep rushing to my rescue, Nick? You barely know me. You're not CIA anymore. You're not a cop. You don't even owe me a favor. Why risk getting involved with a killer? And don't go with the overactive protective gene routine. I'm not buying it."

Nick took a deep breath and reached for her hand. She held on tight and his breath caught in his throat. He was still just as turned on by her, but the fierce need to protect her overshadowed even that.

"I don't know the answer to your questions, Jacinth. I just know that protecting you is the most important thing in my life right now."

"Then I guess I'd be a fool to turn down your offer."

"Biggest fool in town," he said, finally managing a smile. "Now get some clothes on before you drive me out of my mind."

She looked at her panties and ran a finger over the border of lace that stretched across the front. "Get over it, Nick. It's not as if I'm naked. I don't have on much more than this when I'm wearing a bathing suit."

That was a bathing suit he'd pay to see. But if she touched herself like that again, they might both end up naked. He absolutely could not go there.

She strode past him, near enough to touch, though he didn't dare. He turned away.

"Do you want to see this or not?"

When he looked again, she was standing at her closet door, thankfully pulling on a robe.

"I'll check it out."

"I'll meet you in the kitchen," she said.

He was good with that.

ICY FEAR SET IN CLEAR down to her bones as Jacinth processed the information from Nick.

Joy Adams, Cecelia Davis, Jewel Benet. Three young women who had disappeared from the French Quarter within months of each other. Joy Adams had been murdered by a madman. It didn't take a detective to figure out that Cecelia and Jewel might well have met the same fate.

But strangely, instead of making her want to flee the house that had been in the Villaré family for generations, these new revelations made her determined to stay. She was still frustrated and afraid. But now she was also angry, spitting tacks and stamping spiders kind of angry.

How dare the monster kill innocent women for his own sick pleasure? How dare he invade this house and use it for committing his ghastly crimes?

How dare he threaten her?

And no matter that Nick had posed the possibility that the murderer might not be the one who'd broken into her house today, she was convinced it was him.

Jacinth was just thankful that Caitlyn was still on her honeymoon and didn't have to go through this. And she was really glad Nick was here. He was her rock, her gorgeous, sexy, brave rock. She didn't fully understand him, but had she known him for three years instead of three days, she couldn't trust him more.

Nick stretched, walked to the counter and refilled his coffee mug. With all the caffeine he'd consumed, she didn't see how he'd get any sleep tonight and she was starting to fade fast.

"There's something in this house he wants," Jacinth said. "Not the portraits Carrie mentioned, because they would have been too large to shove inside the boxes on my closet shelf. Besides, they're already missing."

"He could be looking for the murder weapon," Nick said. "A bloodstained gutting knife or machete, one sharp enough to cut through flesh, muscle and bone."

"If it was here, either Caitlyn or I may have thrown it out. We carried away a lot of junk from the attic. I don't remember that type of knife, but that doesn't mean I didn't trash one."

"A knife could easily have been hidden in the folds of old clothing or blankets," Nick said.

"But why leave that kind of evidence where there was even a chance someone could find it when he could just as easily have buried that with the body?" Jacinth questioned.

"Maybe he was planning on using it again, and then you and Caitlyn moved in and he didn't get the chance."

"It may not be a weapon he's looking for. He could have known my grandmother personally. She might have even promised him something and then forgot to include it in the will."

"Which leads me to the rest of my story." Nick reached into his pocket, pulled out an antique brooch and set it on the kitchen table between them.

"That looks exactly like the one Carrie Marks described."

"Except this one is a gift from a prince."

"Is the prince responsible for your lumps and bruises?"

"He could be."

Jacinth listened while Nick replayed the Sarah Livingston rendezvous. There was a lot to cover for one brief meeting. Eric Ladeaux. A mysterious prince. And the shoe box full of jewelry he'd obtained only to lose again when someone had clubbed him from behind and sent him tumbling down the steep steps.

Her stomach rolled. "You could have been killed."

"But I wasn't."

"Did you actually go to the hospital and get that head wound checked out? Don't lie to me, Nick."

"I went to the hospital, not in an ambulance like the woman who owned the antique shop and apartments wanted me to do, but I did let her drive me there."

"No wonder I couldn't get you on the phone."

"I would have called you back, but somehow I lost my phone in the fall. I called and reported it stolen. I'll pick up a new one tomorrow."

After all he'd been through today on her account, he'd still come over, sat on her porch and waited for her to get home. And now he was here, ready to put his life on the line to protect her. A crazy kind of warmth flooded her senses.

She'd love to crawl into his arms right now, but even if he held her close for a few breathless minutes, he'd end up pushing her away.

"Were there any expensive jewels included in your grandmother's estate?" Nick asked.

"None than I've come across or were listed in the will, but then the paintings weren't listed, either. My grandmother left Caitlyn and me the house and all its furnishings. She may have decided that was enough for granddaughters who were virtual strangers."

Jacinth picked up the brooch. It was truly beautiful. "I think we should have this appraised."

"What we really need to know is if it was stolen from your grandmother, and, if so, by whom. If we found that out, I think we'd have our killer."

"There is one other thing I should mention," Jacinth said, "though it didn't seem important at the time."

Nick's expression turned grim. "Everything's important now."

"I walked out on the second-story veranda last night for a breath of fresh air. I saw a man standing in front of the B and B who looked to be staring right at me. After a few minutes, he walked away. That's all."

He put his hand over hers and his thumb traced her knuckles. "If it happens again, I'll be here. I'm yours, twenty-four/seven, if you want me, but definitely anytime there's any risk at all. I'll drive you to work in the morning and pick you up when you're ready to leave."

"Dr. Jefferies won't like your cutting into his time," she teased, trying to lighten the moment. At least she made a stab at teasing. She was so tired her words slurred.

She leaned over and laid her head on top of her arms. "Where are you going to sleep, Nick?"

"In the bedroom closest to you. If you make a peep, I'll hear you."

"There's room in my bed. I promise I won't attack you, unless I do it in my sleep."

"But faced with temptation like that, I can't promise I wouldn't attack you."

Nick kept talking, but she closed her eyes and his words floated aimlessly in her mind until they drifted away. Somewhere in the fog, Nick wrapped his arms around her and Jacinth knew she was safe.

JACINTH BARELY STIRRED when Nick lifted her in his arms. He carried her up the wide staircase beneath the canopy of nymphs and satyrs that danced about the cracked and peeling plaster of the ceiling's fresco.

He suspected she hadn't fallen into a sound sleep

since the night he responded to her scream. Fatigue had finally caught up with her.

She was light in his arms and the wisps of hair that brushed his face and neck smelled of springtime. He'd have given anything to meet her under other circumstances. But, like Ron Greene had pointed out to him, even in the best of circumstances, she was way out of his league.

Wine in crystal stems to his beer in a longneck bottle.

Polite where he was blunt.

Soft where he was hard.

He tossed back the covers with one hand and eased Jacinth into bed. She was still in the silk robe. He debated tugging it off her shoulders but decided against it. A glimpse of her bare breasts would start the hunger for her churning inside him again. There was a limit to how much he could take.

He walked to the door and flicked off the light.

"Nick."

"Go back to sleep, Jacinth. I'll be right here."

"There are clean sheets in the hall closet, but none of the beds are made."

"Don't worry about me. Just get some sleep and I'll be here when you wake up, or before that if you need me."

"I do."

"You do what?"

"Uh-huh. You can sleep with me. I have a big bed."

She was lost in the world between drowsiness and dreaming, her words drawn out and slurred. She had no idea what she was offering.

Still the invitation to crawl between the sheets with her and hold her close was the most tempting invitation he'd ever received.

He felt like a rat for not leveling with her now, but that door had closed. Jacinth needed his protection and if she found out who he really was, who his father was, she'd never accept his protection.

If he found evidence that implicated her mother in Micah's murder while proving his father's innocence, she'd hate him for the rest of her life.

There was no way for a happy ending between him and Jacinth. The best he could hope for was keeping her alive.

Chapter Nine

He stood among the twisted roots of the oak tree and stared at the house. Bathed in moonlight and ghostly shadows, it stirred the memories that kept him going. He'd had his best moments there—and some of his worst. Joy Adams fell somewhere in between.

The house had turned on him now, spitting out Joy's head and contaminating his victories. The cops were salivating, but the remains of the dead would never be enough evidence to tie him to the crimes.

Unfortunately, now that Nick Bruno was sleeping with Jacinth, getting in and out of the house would not be as easy as it had been before.

He'd have to move stealthily, choose his opportunities well and always be prepared to kill if it came to that.

Killing had been on his mind a lot lately. The urges grew stronger every day. And now his murderous fantasies always starred the beautiful Jacinth Villaré.

One day her prince would come.

He took one last puff of his cigarette, then snubbed it out with the toe of his shoe and walked away.

Chapter Ten

By one on Tuesday afternoon, Nick had picked up a new phone, had replaced the locks on every door that opened to the outside of the house, made sure all the window locks were secure, and trimmed some hedges that obscured the first-floor windows. He'd also called and made arrangements for the house's outdated alarm system to be fully upgraded.

And he'd spent a half hour on the phone with Detective Greene, bringing him up to speed on yesterday's break-in. Greene would be by momentarily to pick up the note and have it checked for fingerprints.

Nick hadn't mentioned his informative chat with Sarah Livingston or his crashing departure from her apartment.

She'd asked to remain anonymous and he'd grant her that.

He had called Ron Greene and suggested he check into Eric Ladeaux as a possible suspect. Told him word on the street was that Eric and Joy were ex-lovers. He knew Ron would verify that if it was true.

The police already had the prince angle from last

fall's interrogation of Sarah, information they'd ignored at the time.

Now Nick had an hour to shower, pick up Jacinth from Tulane and keep the appointment he had with Jeff Casey at Casey's Gems and Diamonds.

Nick and Casey had been roommates at LSU for two semesters. Jeff was a tell-it-like-it-is kind of guy. Casey's father had been in the jewelry business in the Uptown area for years. Trust and knowledge. Nick figured he was getting the jewelry dream team.

But simply telling him the brooch was worth fifty dollars would amount to no help at all.

JACINTH GLANCED IN THE GLASS cases as they entered the jewelry store, admiring gorgeous necklaces and earrings that she'd never afford on a history professor's salary. Fortunately, that didn't bother her in the least. Having enough money to put a plumber on retainer, however, would be luxury beyond compare.

A slim and sophisticated-looking middle-aged woman looked up and smiled. "Good afternoon. Are you looking for anything special today?"

"We're here to see Jeff," Nick said. "He's expecting us."

"Then you must be Nick Bruno, All-American running back for the Tigers two years in a row."

Nick grinned. "Only because Jeff kept those monster SEC tackles away from me."

"And you must be Jacinth, Marie's granddaughter."

That took Jacinth by surprise. "Did you know Marie?"

"For years. Knew and loved her." She extended a hand. "I'm Eleanor Casey, Jeff's mother."

"I'm so glad to meet you. Actually, I'm glad to meet anyone who knew my grandmother well. I'm still learning about her."

"I only knew Marie as a customer, but she was quite charming. Always pleasant. She spoke of you often. You and your sister. Caitlyn, isn't it?"

"Yes, it's Caitlyn. What types of things did she say about us?"

"Now you're putting me on the spot."

"I don't mean to. It's just that she and my mother had quit speaking years ago, so I can't imagine how Marie kept up with us."

That brought an even bigger smile to Eleanor's lips. "Trust me, Marie had her ways. If it was important to her, she saw that it happened. My husband can attest to that. He and Jeff are expecting you two. Let me tell them that you're here."

Jacinth went back to perusing jewelry.

Nick stepped to her elbow and put his mouth to her ear. "Don't waste your money on this overpriced merchandise. If you're looking for value, I have an antique brooch I can sell you."

"Is it under fifty dollars?"

"Forty-nine ninety-five, plus tax and handling."

"Whatever he's telling you, don't believe him," a male voice cautioned from the back of the store.

"Watch it, bruiser. Don't step on my lines."

Jacinth stood back while the two old college buddies went through the joking and arm-punching routine. But once they'd finished with that and she'd been officially introduced, they quickly got down to business. Jeff led them to the back of the store.

"Dad's the real appraisal expert," Jeff said. "I mostly handle the financial end of the business." He led them over to an older man.

"Dad, meet my buddy Nick Bruno and his friend Jacinth Villaré."

Mr. Casey stood and shook their hands. "I remember you, Nick. We never met, but I watched you make some great game-winning runs for the Tigers."

Nick's football achievement was yet another part of Nick's life that she knew nothing about.

"I knew your grandmother, Jacinth. She drove a hard bargain, that one. Now let me have a look at that brooch you want appraised."

Nick pulled the brooch from his pocket and handed it to Mr. Casey.

Mr. Casey picked up first one and then another of the eye loupes he had lined up on his desk. His mouth was constantly in motion as he studied the brooch, his lips twisting, slanting and puffing out. Jacinth had no idea what any of those expressions meant.

When Mr. Casey returned the last loupe to the table, he scooted his chair away from his desk and looked first at Nick and then at her.

"It's in excellent shape, the stone, the silver, the settings, almost like new though it's been through several generations of the Villaré family."

Nick pushed his chair closer to the desk. "Are you certain it was owned by a Villaré?"

"Absolutely certain. Marie had three of these in her possession at one time, plus the original, that I trust you are keeping in a very safe place, Jacinth."

"What's that copy worth?" Nick asked.

"I gave Luther Villaré twenty thousand dollars for one just like it the year before he was murdered."

Twenty thousand dollars for a brooch Marie had given the woman she thought would be her future daughter-in-law and Carrie had been excited about Luther giving her fifty of that. Jacinth hated to think ill of the dead, but Carrie was lucky to be rid of him.

"I hate to admit it, Mr. Casey, but I'm totally confused by this original/copy discussion," Jacinth said.

"No problem. I'll see if I can clear it up for you. Now I'm going by what Marie told me, so I can't swear to the facts surrounding the original purchase, but I have seen the original and Marie definitely owned it. I appraised it myself and attested to its value when she had it insured. You should have all that information somewhere in the paperwork you received from the attorney who executed her will."

"I don't have any insurance forms."

Nor did she have the original brooch. "Did she keep the brooch in a safe-deposit box?"

"No. I suggested she do just that, but she wouldn't hear of it. She didn't trust banks and she claimed she had the perfect hiding place. Said she'd never told a soul where that was."

"What's the difference between a copy and the original?" Nick asked.

"Sapphires have the same qualifiers as other precious

gems. Size, cut, color, clarity, overall quality, even its geographic origin can affect the price. Right now sapphires from Burma and Kashmir are the most valuable. And once the stone is set into a piece of jewelry, the setting and the reputation of the artist come into play."

"Put it this way," Nick said. "If you put the original next to the copy sitting on your desk right now, would a novice like me be able to tell the difference?"

"As someone who makes my living selling fine jewelry, I'd like to think the differences would be obvious. But if they're not sitting side by side, you might be fooled. Someone familiar with fine jewelry wouldn't. I can promise you that Marie Villaré would instantly notice the difference."

"Did she ever mention how she came to have the original and the copies?" Jacinth asked.

"Only every time she considered selling one of the copies." Mr. Casey chuckled and pushed his eyeglasses up his nose. "She said her mother was so excited when she finally had a girl after four boys and several years of barrenness that her husband splurged and had the original brooch made to celebrate the occasion. That was before the big stock market crash, mind you."

"And the copies?" Nick asked.

"Jonathan Villaré was partial to his sons. So as not to slight them, he had copies of the splendid brooch made for each of his four sons to give their wives when they became engaged, thinking that the original would be passed on from Elizabeth to her beloved daughter, Marie."

"I'd say Jonathan Villaré was a very generous man," Nick said.

"Marie definitely inherited that trait from him, though to put things in perspective, Jonathan paid nowhere near what the brooches are worth today. And, according to Marie, her mother had her own inheritance, so I'm sure the two of them lived quite well."

"Why do you say my grandmother was generous?" Jacinth asked.

"Marie had enough to live on, but only because she lived frugally. But whenever she ran into someone in need, she'd go rummaging in the family jewelry box and come up with a new semiprecious trinket to sell.

"By the time she died, she had little of value left, except the sapphire brooch and the copies, of course. And those, along with the crumbling old Villaré mansion, were to be her legacy to you and Caitlyn."

A legacy that just might get her killed.

"So how much money are we talking with the original?" Nick asked. "A hundred thousand? Two hundred thousand?"

Mr. Casey poked his thumb into the air. "Higher."

"Three hundred thousand?"

"This could take all day."

"So what are we looking at?" Nick insisted.

"Approximately three-quarters of a million dollars, give or take a thousand or two."

"Bingo."

"I can see how my grandmother had the original and the one copy belonging to Nathanial," Jacinth said. "But how did she end up with three copies?"

"She and her husband purchased them from Nat's brothers so that she'd have copies for you, Caitlyn and whoever Luther married."

"What had she planned to do with the original?"

"She never said. I figured it was her insurance policy, in case her money ran out before she died."

And the money had been running out, which was how Jacinth and Caitlyn ended up owing back taxes on the house.

But apparently Marie hadn't sold the brooch, since there hadn't even been enough cash in the estate to pay all the funeral expenses.

So where was the original brooch? And who believed it was rightfully theirs and had threatened to kill Jacinth for it? And why kill three innocent women?

The more answers she discovered, the more confused she became. The mansion was beginning to feel more and more like a nightmare and nothing like home.

JACINTH HAD INSISTED she couldn't eat a bite when Nick pulled into the valet line at Emeril's restaurant. Her mind was in a state of information overload and for some crazy reason she kept picturing the killer as a prince in velvet attire holding a knife in one hand and the sapphire brooch in the other.

As usual, Nick was starving. He ignored her explained lack of appetite and ordered for both of them.

"Whoever left that note is after the original brooch," Nick said as soon as the waiter stepped away. "Whether or not it's actually in the house or not, he believes it is.

What we have to figure out is who knows about the brooch and would feel they're entitled to it."

"Carrie," Jacinth said, saying the first name that popped into her head. "Though she might only be looking for a copy. Marie could have told her she had two more and Luther cheated her out of the brooch that was supposed to go to her."

"Or she could have found out about the original and wants it though it was never hers," Nick said, going along with the theory. "And she's convinced it's hidden somewhere inside the house."

"Because if Marie had told her about the brooch, she might have mentioned it was hidden in a place where no one can ever find it. Only Carrie believes she can."

"There are a few major problems with that theory," Nick said. "One, how is she getting into the house without breaking in?"

"Marie may have shown her a secret passageway."

"Ron Greene was just grasping at straws when he mentioned that yesterday morning."

"Yes, but with all you had to tell me last night, I forgot to tell you about my conversation yesterday with Dr. Jefferies."

"Good old Dr. Jefferies, always there when you need him."

"He's my mentor, Nick. Nothing more, but you are cute when you're jealous."

"I'm not jealous. Tell me about the secret passageway."

She explained about Victoria and her becoming a spy to save Confederate soldiers.

"It sounds extremely likely that the passageway is sealed."

"Likely, but not definite," she said. "At least we need to consider its being a viable entry into the house when we're proposing our theories. Now, what's reason number two?"

The waiter interrupted with a beer, a glass of white wine and an appetizer that quickly changed Jacinth's mind about eating.

"That looks fabulous."

"It's very popular," the waiter said, before leaving them alone again.

"Try it." Nick forked a bite and attempted to feed it to her.

"First, tell me what it is."

"Andouille sausage."

"What's the green stuff?"

"Boy, you *are* a Yankee."

"I was born in New Orleans," she reminded him.

"Then you should know Southern greens when you see them."

"But what kind of Southern greens?"

"Taste it. They'll be so delicious you won't care."

"Translation—you don't know."

She opened her mouth and the delicious mingling of flavors exploded against her taste buds. "Mmm."

"See, a good chef, like a good man, never lets you down."

Nick knew what she'd been through the past few days, what they'd both been through, and that the worst might be still to come. The teasing conversation was his way of keeping her spirits from dragging rock bottom. The amazing thing was that his efforts were working. She took another bite, this one on her own.

"Thanks," she said as the food found its way to her empty stomach.

"For what?"

The reasons that came to mind all sounded mushy or like she was trying to force the relationship again.

"Thanks for knowing how to say *andouille*."

"That's nothing. Wait until I teach you about Boudin."

They finished their appetizer and their entrées and had started on steaming cups of café au lait before the talk went back to sapphire brooches and killers. The relaxed mood faded quickly.

Jacinth sipped her coffee. "You left off at number two on your eliminate-Carrie-as-a-suspect list."

"Refresh my memory. What was one?"

"The question of how she could get into the locked house without breaking in."

"Right. Two—I'm pretty damn sure she's not the one who hammered me yesterday when I was leaving Sarah's apartment. And three, what is her motive for killing Joy Adams?"

Jacinth felt the weight of frustration crushing down on her again, but she just couldn't believe they were dealing with two monsters. One who'd killed Joy Adams and perhaps two other women. Another who was threatening Jacinth for stealing a necklace worth three-quarters of a million dollars.

"Maybe we should start with suspects who might have a motive for murdering Joy Adams."

"You go first," Nick said. "I'll play devil's advocate."

"Based on what you told me Sarah said about Eric Ladeaux, I'd go with him. Joy's jilted lover. Knew Marie well. Had been in this house many times before. If there's a way to sneak in through the attic or loose bricks or some other anomaly, he'd know about it. And for the kicker, he likely knows of the authentic sapphire brooch."

"If he's guilty, who's the prince and how did he get Marie's fake brooch?"

"Maybe that wasn't Marie's. Maybe he really is a foreign prince who fell in love with an American dancer and purchased the brooch that Luther sold to your friend Jeff after he'd started dating Joy."

"That's possible," Nick said reluctantly.

"Then let's hear your top choice."

"Carrie Marks's licentious lover, who was either eavesdropping on our conversation the other night or else had just left for more beer, leaving his chips and dip behind."

"But you didn't see this lover or even know for sure that he exists."

"Nope. Just a hunch on my part."

"But the theory does make sense," she admitted. "Carrie somehow hooked up with a serial killer, maybe through one of those online dating services or just when she was out with her friends.

"She would have talked about Luther, even told him

about Marie's jewels, especially the valuable brooch that might be hidden in the house."

"And mentioned that the house was empty," Nick said.

"The perfect place for him to kill his victims and hide their bodies," Jacinth said. "He may have been searching for the brooch for a while now, but since his crimes have come to light, he has to move quickly. So he leaves me a threatening note to get me out of the house, so that he can find the sapphire brooch."

Nick drained the last drop of his coffee and pushed his cup away. "Are you sure you're not a cop?"

"Just a mystery novel aficionado. We should call Detective Greene."

"All we have is a theory, Jacinth. This is the point where good detective work is all-important."

"And Detective Greene is a detective."

"So am I, and I'd like to handle this as a solo act for now."

"It's too dangerous, Nick. Confronting murder suspects is the NOPD's job. They're trained for situations like this."

"The CIA didn't exactly train me for shooting spitballs."

"Then all we have to do is get the goods on this guy."

"Not *we*. Me. I fly solo."

"If you're going to question Carrie, I'm going with you."

"You're going with me straight back to Casey's Gems and Diamonds. You'll be safe there until I can get to Westwego and back again." Nick signed the credit card receipt the waiter had left when he'd brought their coffee.

"You have a gun."

"More than one," he corrected, "and I'm a crack shot."

"And you said you could protect me. So, prove it, Nick. Prove it at Carrie's house."

"Not happening, because you won't be at Carrie's. C'mon. We're wasting time arguing about this."

She unzipped her handbag, took out her cell phone and started punching in numbers.

"Who are you calling?" he demanded.

"I need to speak with Detective Ron Greene," she bluffed into her phone. "Tell him Jacinth Villaré is calling and that it's extremely—"

Nick grabbed the phone from her hands and broke the connection. He checked the number she'd just dialed— the phone in her cubbyhole office at the university.

Frowning, he slid the phone across the table. She caught it just before it fell into her lap.

"You can go with me," he said, "but if I get there and sense any danger to you at all, we leave and you may have screwed up whatever chance I might have had at snaring Joy's killer. Is that what you want?"

"I want the killer caught at least as badly as you do, Nick. But, for once in my life, I don't want to be the staid and cautious Villaré. I want to go for the gusto. I want to help find the evidence to lock the prince behind bars and get back my house and my life."

"I think I like you better staid—whatever the hell that means. I know I like you better safe."

Chapter Eleven

There were two cars parked in Carrie's driveway. All four doors and the trunk of a light blue compact car were standing open. The trunk was loaded with boxes and one of the older TVs that weighed a ton.

Jacinth peered inside the car as they passed. Every square inch of room except the driver's seat was piled with clothes, boxes and cooking utensils.

"Looks like Carrie has been cleaning out closets," Jacinth said.

"And giving it all away to whoever drives the blue compact."

"Do you suppose that she and Prince Charming are running scared and making a run for it even before they get their hands on the sapphire?"

"Would be smart for him if he's guilty and doesn't want to rot in prison, but difficult for me to believe he's taking Carrie with him. I figured that if this mystery man is Joy's killer that he was only using Carrie to get to the sapphire."

A shiver of apprehension slithered up Jacinth's spine

in spite of her earlier bravado. "Do you think the boy-friend is here?"

"We don't even know for certain there is a boy-friend."

Nick had a finger poised to ring the bell when the door opened and a plump woman wearing jeans a size too small started backing onto the narrow porch. Her arms were loaded down with pillows. Nick stepped out of her path.

"Good thing this is my last load," the woman called to someone inside the house. "I'll have to squash them down to half their size to get the back door closed."

"Here, let me help you with those," Jacinth offered.

The woman spun around and looked from Jacinth to Nick. "I didn't see y'all out here. It's a wonder I didn't back right over you. Hope you're not here for the give-aways. I think I cleared Carrie out."

"We're just here to see Carrie," Nick said. "Does she have more company?"

"Not now. Bertha and Mattie just left. They dropped by to bring Carrie a going-away gift. Cafeteria's not going to be the same without our Carrie cutting up the way she does."

The woman mashed the top pillow down with her chin and used her toe to feel for the drop-off from the porch to the first step.

"Hand me two of those before you fall," Jacinth said, this time with authority.

"Maybe I better." The woman shared the load and called back to Carrie. "You've got more company, hon. You're never going to get through packing."

Jacinth looked through the open door and spied two large suitcases and a plaid carry-on bag stacked next to the sofa. And evidently there was at least one more piece of luggage still being filled.

Carrie was definitely leaving town and likely for good. Whether or not there was a man involved with the move was yet to be proved, though Jacinth was pretty much convinced that there was.

By the time Jacinth made it back to the porch, Carrie was at the door.

"What a surprise," Carrie said. "Didn't expect to see you two again before I left town."

"I didn't realize you were moving," Nick said.

"I didn't realize it myself until yesterday. My aunt in California fell and broke her hip and she needs me to help with her housecleaning business."

The pillow lady stepped over and slid an arm around Carrie's waist. "She'll make twice as much money on the West Coast as she does here. Plus she'll have free room and board at her aunt's house."

"Which is three times as big as this one," Carrie said. "With a pool." She did a sexy pirouette. "And Janie, here, and all my friends from school can come out for a visit."

"I'm going to start saving for my plane ticket tomorrow," Janie said. "And I better get out of here before I start crying." She and Carrie fell into a bear hug. Janie left after that without looking back.

"I wish I could stand around and talk to you about your grandmother for hours," Carrie said, "but I really do have to get back to my packing."

"Do you mind if Jacinth uses your bathroom before we go?" Nick said. "She's got this itty-bitty kidney and has to go every time I get in rush-hour traffic. Women."

Itty-bitty kidney problem? You'd think a trained CIA agent could come up with something better than that. Besides, she had no idea what he expected her to do inside the house.

Look for a killer? Steal Carrie's email password? Excellent idea. Too bad she had no idea how.

The first glitch in Carrie's performance showed in a mild expression of irritation, but she didn't refuse the request. "No problem. C'mon in, Jacinth. I'll show you where the bathroom is."

"I'll go back and wait in the car," Nick said. "Don't stay in there all day the way you usually do, Jacinth."

She decoded that to mean she should take her time, so maybe he was the one who was supposed to snoop. Jacinth stayed in the bathroom long enough to read a complete article in the copy of *People* magazine that was sitting on the edge of the tub.

When she'd thanked Carrie, said her goodbyes and left the house, Nick was waiting in the car as he said, engine running.

Jacinth slid into the passenger seat. "What do we do now?"

"Breathe easy."

He handed her a sheet of paper with flight information and the name Billy Raquet scribbled on it. The flight was for tomorrow morning to Belize.

"Carrie is not going to California and not going alone."

She was still puzzled. "How did you get this?"

"Mostly luck. I found the e-tickets in the side pocket of the plaid bag while you were gone. I've already called Detective Greene with the information."

"Is this enough proof to get Billy Raquet arrested?"

"This and the outstanding warrant for his arrest on burglary charges in Shreveport are enough to get him arrested. They're not enough to keep him in jail or to prove he killed Joy Adams, but at least Greene can stop Raquet and Carrie from leaving the country."

"How did you get that information so quickly?"

"Secret powers of a good P.I.—and the computer Greene was sitting in front of when we talked. Is there anything you'd like to do while we're out?"

"No, I just want to go home and spend an evening with you worried about absolutely nothing at all. Unfortunately, I still have a class to teach."

Jacinth had dismissed her night class early and Nick had met her at the door and walked her to his truck. Now they were back at her house and Jacinth seemed to be slowly unwinding from the events of the past few days.

The only light in the comfortable den was the soft glow from a cluster of scented candles on the coffee table. A CD of hauntingly romantic trumpet solos played softly in the background. Jacinth was snuggled next to him on the sofa, not talking, simply cuddling in his arms.

A man could live a lifetime and never have life feel this right. But this was only an illusion, one that would disappear as soon as Nick knew for certain that the danger to Jacinth was past. That could be a matter of hours.

It made the elation over Billy Raquet's looming arrest bittersweet.

Jacinth scooted down so that she was lying on the sofa with her head resting in his lap. "I keep thinking about my mother and how she set out all alone with two little girls, Caitlyn only an infant, rather than stay in this house."

His muscles tightened and feelings of guilt swelled in his chest. Not guilt for wanting to clear his father's name but for the lies that lay between him and Jacinth. Still, he couldn't back away from this conversation.

"Why do you think she left?"

"I always thought it was because she couldn't face living here without my father. Now I'm not so sure. I know how I felt the other night when I wanted to storm out of here and never come back."

"It was different for you. Your life was threatened."

"Mother could have felt threatened, too. She may have thought the man who killed my father would come after her. She might have seen or heard something that put her in danger. And her dying would have left Caitlyn and me without either of our parents."

"Did she meet someone new?"

"No. I don't remember her even dating until I was in the sixth grade."

"If she had dated when you first moved to Ohio, you wouldn't remember it. You were only two."

Jacinth pulled away from him and sat up straight. "You're doing it again, Nick. Every time I mention my mother you make some negative comment. What do you have against mothers, or is it against women in general?"

"I didn't mean to be negative."

"Well, you were. My mother loved my father and she loved Caitlyn and me. She didn't run off with another man and she didn't latch onto the first one she met. She raised us all by herself with no help from anyone."

"Then you should be proud of her."

"I am. And now that I'm back in New Orleans, I plan to learn all I can about my father's killer. I know he's still in prison now, and if his name comes up for parole, I'll fight it."

"Maybe you should meet the man first."

"Maybe I will. All of sudden, I'm really tired, so if you'll excuse me, Nick, I'm going to bed."

Nick watched her walk away. He ached to go after her, to take her in his arms and carry her to bed the way he had last night. Only this time he wanted to crawl in her bed with her and make love to her all night long. And then he'd wake up in the morning and start all over again.

That was a nice dream. But it was never going to be.

Nick's mind shifted gears, plunging him back in the pages upon pages of transcripts from the trial that had found his father guilty of murder. He'd been over the file so often since leaving the CIA that he could quote huge segments from memory.

Regardless of what he'd told Jacinth and others, proving his father's innocence had been Nick's real impetus for leaving the CIA. He'd given up on finding a procedural flaw that would nullify the jury's findings. What he needed was conclusive evidence that pointed to the real killer.

A person with opportunity and motive. A person who'd demonstrated erratic behavior patterns following the murder. Sophie Villaré fit the mold perfectly.

Luther Villaré had testified in court that he'd heard Sophie and Micah arguing the day of the murder. Even Marie had admitted that Sophie seemed distraught that night.

But she'd provided the alibi Sophie needed to keep from becoming a suspect. Marie had testified that Sophie had not left the Villaré house that she and Micah and their two young children shared with Marie.

Sophie had moved out of the house just hours after the ripped and chewed remnants of Micah's clothes were discovered in the alligator-infested bayou where he'd gone fishing with his best friend, who just happened to be Nick's father. She hadn't even bothered to return for the memorial service.

Even Nick's father had admitted that Sophie was constantly on Micah's case to move away from his family and New Orleans. But he'd also stressed that he'd never seen two people more in love than Micah and Sophie. Elton refused to believe that Sophie could have had anything to do with the murder.

Nonetheless, Nick was convinced that Sophie had either been directly involved in the murder or at least knew what had happened that night. It was the only explanation for her strange behavior in running so fast and separating herself so completely from the Villarés.

Nick was determined to find the truth. He'd do that for his father. But right now, all he could think of was keeping Jacinth safe.

And how much he wished he could hold her in his arms tonight.

JACINTH WOKE to the piercing ring of her phone. She rubbed her eyes until she could open them enough to see the clock by her bed. Six o'clock. No one ever called that early with good news.

Still half asleep, she fumbled around until her fingers closed around the phone.

"Hello."

"Did I wake you?"

"Who is this?"

"Detective Greene. I hated to call so early but I wanted to be sure I caught you before you left for school."

"This is my late morning. No classes until ten o'clock. If this is bad news, take two aspirin and call me after nine."

"What if it's good news?"

"Then you can call after seven. Just kidding. Please tell me you've arrested Billy Raquet and that he's confessed to everything. I need to know that he'll spend the rest of his life in jail and never have the opportunity to kill again."

"He's been arrested—at the airport. We couldn't locate him until he showed up for his flight that we knew about thanks to Nick's and your investigative work."

"Thank you."

"Raquet hasn't confessed to anything, but Carrie is doing some serious blabbing, mostly about Raquet's crimes. She admits to going to the Villaré house with him several times while it was empty but says all they stole was some worthless jewelry that the pawnshop wouldn't even deal with them on.

"She suspects that Raquet stole some of your grand-mother's paintings on his own, but insists that she had nothing to do with that. She doesn't admit to knowing anything about Joy Adams's murder."

"What's her motive for squealing on her boyfriend?"

"When she got to the airport this morning, she learned that he'd canceled her ticket."

"So he was leaving the country without her. Nick thought that's what he'd do. Did Carrie explain how they got into the house without breaking a lock?"

"Apparently picking locks is one of Raquet's special-ties. He's also a whiz at disarming alarm systems and cutting plate-glass windows. He's been in and out of jail for theft since he was seventeen."

"That's a big jump from theft to luring women into a vacant house to kill and decapitate them."

"The sad truth is, people cross those thin lines every day. That's why my job never slows down."

When Jacinth concluded her conversation, she called the university. She needed that personal emergency leave Dr. Jefferies had mentioned. Not an extended one, just for a couple of days. She needed closure so that she could move on.

And while she was at it, she'd call Jefferies and ask

him how to get in touch with Dr. Eugenia Kibecti. A secret passageway might be the perfect place to hide a valuable brooch. Even if the passageway had been sealed at one time, that didn't guarantee that Marie hadn't had it reopened.

Jacinth was determined to find that brooch, most likely without Nick's help, since he seemed determined to push her away. She hated the thought of losing him before they ever had a chance to see what they could be together.

He was the first man she'd ever met she thought she could fall in love with. In fact, she probably already had, though falling so hard and fast went against every rule of prudence she'd ever established for herself.

JACINTH'S EFFORTS AT FALLING back asleep failed, so she pulled on her most comfortable pair of old jeans and topped them with an emerald-green sweater. She didn't bother with a bra. At this point she figured she could walk around the house stark naked without having Nick jump her bones.

She knew she turned him on. She wasn't blind. She could see the bulge in his jeans, even at times when she least expected it. Evenings when her hair was wet from the shower and early in the morning when she'd come down for coffee without even brushing her teeth.

He might drool. He didn't succumb. And whatever his reasons were for pulling away from the passion that had burned in those first few kisses, he wasn't sharing it with her. He'd rather push her away with irritating comments about her mother, anything to keep from getting close.

The smell of coffee drifted up from the kitchen. Nick was up and stirring. She should go down and tell him about the detective's call. Their killer was behind bars. The danger was over. Nick was free to go back to his own apartment, back to his own life.

"You don't look ready to be chauffeured to class this morning."

"I'm taking a few days' leave."

"That's a great idea. What shall we do? Go for a walk? Take a drive? Go fishing?"

"That's an idea. I've never been fishing."

"Then I'll have you down to my bayou hideaway one day. You can sit on the front porch and watch silver-finned fish jump six feet out of the water. Or you can drop a line and cork, open a beer and just sit back and enjoy the quiet until you see that cork start bobbing."

He pantomimed the actions as he talked, his muscles flexing as he pulled his imaginary catch into his imaginary boat. She loved listening to him talk. He had that Big Easy way about him that made her feel she was in a world apart from university life.

Not that she wanted to exchange her world for his. It was the dynamics of the two that intrigued her. Or else it was just being with Nick that made her feel so alive.

She joined the game with him, dropping her line into the water and then pulling it in, jumping out of the way of the imaginary fish as it flopped about in her pretend pirogue. "Now what do I do with this slimy creature?"

"Clean it, woman, and I'll fry it up with some hush

puppies and potatoes and we'll have us a feast. Then we'll just sit back, watch the moon come up and keep an eye on a couple of lazy gators floating down the bayou."

"I was ready to go with you until you brought up the lazy gators. Now I'm afraid I have to nix the whole idea."

"And here I was hoping I'd found a woman who'd clean my fish for me."

"Dream on."

Nick pulled two mugs from the shelf above the coffeepot and filled them both, handing one to her.

"I had a phone call from Detective Greene this morning," she said.

"I wondered who was calling that early when I heard your phone ring."

"I'm sorry it woke you."

"It didn't. I woke up about three and couldn't get back to sleep."

"Thinking about our success with pinpointing Carrie's boyfriend as Joy's killer?"

"Concerned that it came too easy and that the square pegs went too quickly into round holes."

"I'm not following you."

"It's easy to connect the dots when you have the pattern already pictured in your mind. But you may not always get the true picture."

"If you're worried that we're participating in lynching the wrong man, I can probably ease those concerns." She dropped into a kitchen chair and shared the details of Detective Greene's phone call.

"I guess that means you're relieved of protective custody duty," she said.

"Are you trying to get rid of me?"

"I thought you'd be eager to get back to your P.I. practice. You must have investigations you should oversee."

"Nothing that can't wait until Greene finds concrete evidence to link Raquet with Joy Adams's murder. Stealing paintings and buying a ticket to Belize just doesn't seal the deal for me."

Nick's expressed concerns added to the doubts Jacinth was already experiencing. She was glad he was staying, even though every day they were together would make it that much harder when he moved out.

"I'll cook breakfast," Nick said.

"I'll start searching every nook and cranny in this sprawling mansion and see if I can find the entrance to a secret passageway or a silver-and-sapphire brooch worth three-quarters of a million dollars."

"What will you do if you find it? Keep the brooch or sell it?"

"It would belong to Caitlyn and me, so I'd only get half a vote."

"What would you do with your portion—if you sold it?"

"Get the plumbing fixed. And build another kitchen so that Caitlyn and Marcus could have completely separate living quarters and a lot more privacy when they return from their honeymoon."

Sin pranced into the kitchen as if she'd been called to an audience of her adoring public.

"You now, Sin, if I ever found out that you'd swallowed that sapphire, I'd throw this can opener away and you'd be forced to eat the cheapest cat food on the market."

Undaunted, Sin utilized her menacing, yellow-eyed stare to prove she wasn't afraid of threats.

Jacinth sighed and opened the can. "In my next life, I'm coming back as a cat."

Then she wouldn't need anybody, not even a tomcat named Nick.

AFTER FIVE HOURS of crawling into narrow, low spaces, straining to reach high ones and helping Nick check inside massive light fixtures, Jacinth was approaching the state of utter and absolute mental devastation.

Busting her toe with a dropped screwdriver she was using to scrape across the top of a window ledge was the last straw. She was going to take a shower and go to work. At least at the university, she'd be doing something useful. She started up the stairs and stopped on the landing.

"You could help me out here, Victoria. Just give me a sign." Victoria maintained the same stern, condescending stare she'd held for generations.

Jacinth dropped to the step, propped her elbows against her knees and rested her head in her hands. The truth hit her slowly. Her frustration wasn't about the brooch or the money. It was about the bodies that might be buried in her walls.

She kept pushing the dreaded images to the back of her mind, but even when she didn't acknowledge them, they were there, like black gaping holes waiting to pull her in.

Not one body, but at least three. The police might not have proof, but Jacinth knew they were there. The musky stench of death that permeated the family tomb lived inside these walls, occasionally reaching out to choke her.

Her home, her legacy, was a morgue.

And the killer was going to come for her.

Shudders attacked and Jacinth started to shake uncontrollably. At some level she knew it was only the stress overtaking her. She had to pull herself together.

Still, tears rolled down her cheeks.

"Jacinth, what's wrong?"

She closed her eyes as Nick's strong arms wrapped around her.

"He killed them in this house, Nick. They were young and alive. They had dreams and hopes. And a monster took that all from them for his own sick pleasure."

The shudders and sobs started again. Nick cradled her in his arms and rocked her like a baby.

"It's okay," he crooned. "It's okay."

When she finally stopped crying, she looked up at Nick. His shirt was wet from her tears. "We should have gone fishing," she whispered.

He smiled, and then his lips touched hers. The kiss was sweeter than before, loving and protective, yet still rife with passion.

He stood and tugged her to her feet. His fingers tangled in her hair and his hands splayed across her back. And then in a sweeping motion he picked her up and carried her up the stairs.

The doorbell rang just as they reached the door to her bedroom.

"I'm not expecting anyone," she whispered. "Don't answer and they'll go away."

"NOPD," a foghorn blared.

"Something big is up," Nick said, as he let her slide down his body until her feet kissed the Persian rug. "That's not your friendly officer's way of getting your attention."

And then he bounded down the stairs, leaving her to deal with swollen eyes, a runny nose, the next trauma and a desire that even in the face of disaster just wouldn't quit.

EMOTIONALLY RATTLED by his love-starved body and the increased guilt he was feeling about lying to Jacinth, Nick yanked open Jacinth's front door. "I hope you clowns have a good reason for alerting the whole neighborhood of your presence."

A cop he'd never met waved a piece of paper as if it were a flag he expected Nick to salute.

"We have a warrant to search the house and grounds of the property at this address belonging to Ms. Jacinth Villaré. The occupants are not forced to leave the property unless they fail to follow the direct commands of one of the officers conducting the search."

"It's about time you guys made it. I'll inform Ms. Villaré that you're here."

And then he'd take a very cold shower and see if he could fit his own head back on straight.

Chapter Twelve

He watched the excitement from his usual spot beneath the gnarly oak tree. Normally, he only visited the vicinity of his private morgue in the darkness, but the flurry of activity today was too stimulating to miss.

And being here in the daylight would be all the better for catching a glimpse of Jacinth. She reminded him so very much of her father. She had Micah's Creole fire in her blood. Had his eyes, so dark they looked like puddled ink. Had his hair, thick and dark as a moonless night.

That's why taking her life would be his most thrilling kill to date. He would have her in his hands begging for mercy and pleading with him to let her live. And it would bring back that delicious rush of exhilaration he'd felt when he'd slit Micah's throat.

The police were congratulating themselves over their coffee and doughnuts this morning, pleased that they'd found their killer.

But the joke would be on them.

He needed that sapphire in the worst way. It was rightfully his. He'd more than earned it. Luckily he didn't have to wait until he'd found it to escape with Jacinth to his walk of twisted fame. If he had to kill Nick Bruno, well, it was only something he should have done years ago.

The urges were on the verge of explosion, the way they had been last fall when he'd killed three women much too close together.

He couldn't put gratification off much longer. Tonight might have to be the night.

Chapter Thirteen

Jacinth watched as the small army of police officers swarmed like hungry termites, dismantling the house piece by piece. The bathroom where the nightmare had started was the focus of destruction, but no area of the house was left untouched.

Ceiling tiles were removed from one room, selected floorboards from another. Rugs were rolled up and pushed aside. Furniture was rearranged like a kid with a new set of blocks. If there was method to their madness, it was not apparent to Jacinth.

Her cell phone rang and she had to search through rolls of protective plastic to find it.

"Hello."

"Hi, Jace. It's me, Caitlyn."

"Good to hear from you."

"Guess where Marcus and I are going tomorrow."

"On a boat ride."

"No. I'll give you a hint."

"Can't you just tell me?"

"What's wrong?" Caitlyn asked.

"Nothing. Why would you think something is wrong?"

"Your voice has that twang you get when you're stressed."

Super. Now she had a twang *and* an itty-bitty bladder. Her body was collapsing at a pace with the house.

"Of course I'm not stressed. Why would I be stressed?"

"Because you need a man in your life, someone wonderful and exciting—like my Marcus."

"Can't imagine where I'd find a wonderful, exciting, sexy man around here."

"I didn't say anything about sexy."

"Then I'll remove that from my checklist. Where are you and Marcus going tomorrow?"

"To St. Martin."

Jacinth winced as two skinny cops lifted the huge portrait of Victoria from the wall and half dropped, half set it against the side wall. Victoria bobbled but didn't fall.

"St. Martin?" Jacinth repeated, trying to get her mind back in the conversation. "Is that a church?"

"No. St. Martin, the island. It's in the northeast Caribbean."

"Oh, that St. Martin. Sounds fun."

"We met this wonderful couple who own a very exclusive galley there and they're flying us down. They're interested in featuring a display of Marcus's work."

"You can't just fly off with a couple you just met. They might—"

"Relax, Jace. You don't have to watch over me. I'm

all grown up. So is Marcus. We had the couple checked out. They and their galley are legit. But we'll be gone a couple of extra days. I just wanted to let you know."

"No problem. Stay gone as long as you want." *Because you definitely don't want to hurry back for this.*

"We're breaking up," Jacinth lied. It was impossible to communicate with Caitlyn in the midst of the chaos. "Love you and take care."

"Love you, too."

Jacinth put down the phone and studied the now crooked Victoria and her commanding appearance even leaning against the wall like a drunken queen. Victoria the brave overseer of the Villaré mansion.

The perfect person to guard the beloved brooch.

Not a half-bad concept. So obvious in fact that Jacinth should have thought of it from the first.

Anticipation rippled through her as she ran to find Nick. She didn't trust herself to handle the heavy picture without help. She found him standing at the door to her bedroom, glaring at the two young cops searching under her bed as if he dared them to make a wrong move.

She coerced him into going with her and, in minutes, the two of them were carefully removing the protective backing from the portrait.

"Don't put too much faith in this agenda," Nick cautioned.

"Don't worry. I've had my meltdown for the day, and one's my limit."

"If the brooch isn't here, that doesn't mean you won't find it," Nick reminded her, when they were nearly done removing the backing. "Mr. Casey seemed certain the brooch was insured."

"It's not about urgency or the money," she assured him.

"Then why are we going at this in the middle of an invasion when we'll have the house to ourselves in a few hours?"

"It just seems the perfect hiding place and I have to keep doing something or go crazy."

They removed the last of the backing and then lay the canvas flat, shoving poor Victoria's face into the floor. Jacinth poked her fingertips into each corner not once but twice. She'd been so certain the brooch would be here.

"Nothing," she murmured.

"Sorry, Jacinth."

"I'm starting to hate this house and the brooch."

"When all this is past, you'll love them both."

"*If* this passes."

She tried to step out onto the veranda for a breath of fresh air and some privacy, but only made it to the door.

"Ms. Villaré."

She turned to the young officer who'd addressed her.

"Detective Greene would like to talk to you in the kitchen."

"I didn't realize he was here."

"Yes, ma'am. We called him. He just arrived a few minutes ago."

If they'd called the lead detective, it must mean they'd found important evidence. Jacinth hurried to the kitchen. Greene was grim-faced as always, but this time there was a hardness in his face and neck she hadn't noticed before.

"Have you found new evidence?"

He nodded. "We've found two full bodies and what we believe is the remainder of Joy Adams's body."

Jewel, Cecelia and Joy. They weren't formally identified as yet, but Jacinth knew it was them.

All dead. All murdered. All entombed in the walls of her and Caitlyn's new home.

Jacinth's stomach lurched and she ran for the back door, reaching the yard just in time to lose her breakfast in the dirt.

NICK SEARCHED UNTIL HE SPOTTED Jacinth standing on the porch with her head cradled in her hands. He'd hoped she wouldn't have to face this, but he was relieved the police had found the bodies.

Family members needed closure. Knowing was hard. Not knowing was even harder. He'd call Jewel's father as soon as the victims' IDs were official. He'd take it hard. Hell, Nick was taking it hard and he was supposed to be a tough, insensitive private detective.

Nick joined Jacinth and put his arm around her shoulder.

"You heard?" she asked.

"Yeah. Are you holding up okay?"

"I'm a bit numb. The concept of one young woman being murdered and left to rot in this house is gruesome. The confirmation that it's three is almost inconceivable."

"Have you thought about going back to work for the rest of the day? It would occupy your mind and might be better than hanging around here."

"I can't face work. I would like to get out of here for a while, though."

"My truck's on ready. Just point me in the right direction."

"I'll need to make a phone call first."

"I'm ready anytime."

EUGENIA KIBECTI GREETED Nick and Jacinth graciously and invited them into her home. She was tall and willowy, with auburn hair cut into a chin-length bob. Her ankle-length flowered skirt was topped by a tailored white cotton blouse.

Jacinth's first impression upon crossing the threshold was that she'd stepped into a museum. Not only did the furnishings appear to be genuine antiques, but every accessory, light fixture, picture and even the arrangements of fresh flowers seemed authentic to the period.

"You've done an amazing job with the house," Jacinth said.

"Thank you. We try. My husband Bill and I have spent years acquiring just the right pieces. We're both American history buffs."

"That shows."

"The house was practically in ruins when we bought it—which is the only way we could have afforded it. That and the fact that Bill made the *New York Times* bestseller list for the first time that year."

"William Kibecti, historical mystery writer," Nick

said. "Now I know why the name Kibecti sounded familiar."

Eugenia smiled. "Have you read his books?"

"Several of them. I'm not a big reader of fiction, but your husband is one of my dad's favorite writers, and he got me hooked. Dad never mentioned Kibecti lived in New Orleans, though."

"Bill tries to keep a low profile in his private life."

"I can see why," Jacinth said, realizing it was the first time Nick had mentioned his father. "I really appreciate your letting us drop by this afternoon."

"No problem. Reggie Jefferies said you and your sister inherited the Villaré mansion on Esplanade. That's long been one of my favorites. It has such character."

"Yes," Jacinth agreed, "but we have a long way to go before it's fully restored."

"These old houses are always a work in progress. But your house is well worth the trouble for its historic significance alone. Victoria Villaré was quite the Confederate heroine."

"Actually, in a roundabout way, she's the reason I'm here. I'm trying to locate the secret passageway Victoria used to spy on Union officers, but I don't really know what I'm looking for. Dr. Jefferies thought you might be able to help."

"Did Reggie also tell you that Bill took him on a tour through Bill's secret, narrow chamber once?"

"No, he didn't mention that."

"You should definitely ask him about it. I don't think I've seen a man turn exactly that shade of green before."

They all turned toward the doorway to spot the source of the deep male voice.

"My husband, Bill," Eugenia said.

Bill was thin and wiry with hair just beginning to gray at the temples. He looked to be a few years older than Eugenia, probably somewhere in his mid-fifties. He was dressed in khaki chinos and a long-sleeved striped polo shirt. His only outstanding physical feature was his mischievous smile.

They introduced themselves all around and shook hands. Once that was done, Nick and Bill engaged in a spirited discussion of the complexities and denouement in Bill's latest novel. Yet another side to Nick she'd never seen before. He constantly amazed her.

"How did you discover the entrance to the passageway?" Jacinth asked at the first break in conversation.

"By accident," Bill admitted. "And it actually wasn't the original entrance I found since it had been sealed off. I was removing a built-in bookcase and part of the wall came down with it. And there was the passageway, just behind the crumbling wall."

Bill got a passageway. She got bodies. Jacinth shuddered as that fact hit home again.

"The passageways have shifted over time in these old houses," Bill said. "It can make for some surprising discoveries when new owners attempt major renovations. I remember after one hurricane a few years back, a box of silver pieces fell through a man's roof. It was the first he knew of a second-floor passageway."

And after a water leak in her walls, bodies had been

discovered in the Villaré bathroom. Who knew what other horrors might be waiting for her and Caitlyn?

"Our passageway has shifted so much that it's barely a crawlspace in some areas," Bill said. "And so narrow in others that on my first investigation, I nearly became lodged between two support beams."

"That sounds familiar," Nick said.

"Ah, you do know my work. How about a tour of the passageway? Don't worry. I've bolstered the walls and ceilings so that nothing will cave in on you."

"I'd love that," Jacinth said.

"I don't recommend it," Eugenia said. "At least not for you, Jacinth."

"Why not?"

"Bill has a taste for the macabre, and I've left him to his own whims with the passageway."

"Historical possibility, but not recommended for the weak stomach," Bill agreed. "Jefferies will vouch for that."

A cold shiver climbed Jacinth's spine. But it couldn't be more frightening than what she'd already faced.

"I'd like the tour," she said, amazed that her voice didn't give away her trepidation.

Nick placed a hand at the small of her back. "Are you sure? If there's anything there that will help you locate the Villaré passageway, I'll find it for you."

She appreciated his concern, but she felt compelled to do this, almost as if Joy, Cecelia, Jewel and perhaps dozens of other victims were depending on her personally. She knew that was bizarre, but she was here. She had to do this.

"It's perfectly safe," Bill said.

Jacinth met Nick's concerned gaze for an instant and then looked away. He had every reason to think she couldn't handle this. He'd seen her after the head had tumbled down on her and also that day in the cemetery.

"I'll be fine," she said. "It's only a passageway."

So why was her heart threatening to pound its way right out of her chest?

Chapter Fourteen

BILL LED THEM into the first-floor library. He approached what appeared to be a built-in bookcase. Raising to his tiptoes, he reached behind a book on the top shelf and then stepped back. Jacinth watched, amazed, as one section of the bookcase swung open.

"I thought you hadn't found the entrance," Jacinth said.

"Not initially, but I was able to locate it once inside the passageway. It's still sealed. This is a new entrance I had built to my specifications." He put out a hand as if to beckon them into the shadowed burrow. "Shall we?"

"You lead the way," Jacinth insisted.

He did and she followed with Nick close behind since the passageway was only wide enough for one at a time. Even then, it was tight.

Bill aimed a beam of light down the dark passage, illuminating rows of gossamer webs hanging from the low ceiling. A huge spider dangled from one. Gooseflesh dotted Jacinth's arms.

"Where does the passageway lead?" Nick asked.

"It appears that it originally tunneled to the carriage

house that was torn down years ago. That was all sealed off, as well. Now it only goes for fifty-two feet, weaving behind the guest bedrooms and a bath before narrowing to a dead end. That was all I decided to restore."

Bill and the light disappeared around a curve. Nick put a reassuring hand on her shoulder as she hurried to catch up. One glance into the new section and her stomach pitched into a violent roll.

Human bones littered the floor. A few feet in front of her, a hideous mummified body lay scrunched against the wall.

Jacinth took quick breaths, desperately trying not to scream or faint. Still, an icy shudder ripped through her and she almost tripped on a skull. It bounced in front of her, coming to rest against a huge rat.

Nick clasped both her shoulders and pulled her back against his broad chest. "None of this is real, Jacinth. The rat, bones and body are all bogus."

"Absolutely," Bill said. "Well, except for the skull. But definitely not the decaying cadaver. It's all for effect." He picked up a leg bone and tapped against it with his fingernails. "See, hard plastic, purchased online."

Her pulse slowed to somewhere near normal.

"I apologize, Jacinth. I should have explained, but it never occurred to me you'd be fooled by the imitations. Believe me, were they real, I wouldn't venture in here myself, and Eugenia would probably make me sell the house."

"Guess I stole the turning-green record from Dr. Jefferies," she said, trying to make light of her horror.

Not that she wasn't so squeamish that even the fake was still freaking her out.

Bill chuckled. "Reggie knew this was all spurious trappings, and he still couldn't take it. I don't think he'd survive a modern Halloween haunted house."

They turned one more corner, but this time the space was clear. The remainder of the tour was reasonably uneventful, but also another washout. The only knowledge she'd gained that might help was the information about the passageway initially leading to the carriage house.

But it had presented the possibility that she could access the Villaré passageway through the section of wall that had caved in. As yet, Detective Greene had not made that option accessible to her, but eventually he would.

For now, she'd have her work cut out for her just checking every inch of space inside and out of her dilapidated carriage house.

NICK HAD STOPPED at a seafood market for fresh shrimp on the way home and then he'd made the most delicious shrimp fettuccini Jacinth had ever tasted. Her contribution had been a salad and garlic bread. Merely watching him move around her kitchen had been a turn-on.

He talked as he worked, about a past Mardi Gras, the Saints Super Bowl win, his cabin on the bayou—everything except the trauma she was living through.

He fed her tasting bites, kissed sauce from her lips and kept her wineglass full. Nothing seemed forced with him. His charm flowed effortlessly and unrelentingly. Yet, she suspected his efforts were designed to help her relax.

When they finished the meal, they took their drinks to the front porch and settled on the creaking swing. She snuggled close and he slipped an arm around her shoulders.

"Tell me about you, Nick."

"What do you want to know?"

"What you were like as a kid."

"Pretty much like every other kid. I lived on my bike. Fished with my grandpa. Talked too much in class. Played every sport that was offered, but finally settled on football."

"Apparently you were very good at it."

"I did all right until I busted up my knee senior year. Even that worked out for the best. It helped me get my focus back on my studies. I went into the CIA right after graduation and I loved my time with them."

"Any brothers or sisters?"

"No."

"Where are your parents now?"

She felt his muscles tense.

"This is starting to feel like an interrogation."

"I'm just fascinated by you. You're like no one I've ever met before. Smart, protective, sexy, honest…"

She could have gone on and on, but he stopped her with her mouth on hers. The kiss was deliciously exciting and when his right hand cupped her breast, her breath caught in her throat.

His thumb rode her nipple through her clothes. She arched toward him, wanting more, wanting so much more.

When the kiss ended, he pulled away.

"Is there someone else, Nick. If there is, just tell me. It will hurt, but I'll understand."

"There's no one else, Jacinth."

"So you just don't want to be involved with me?"

"I am involved with you."

"Within limits."

"I'm crazy about you, Jacinth. I've told you that."

"Then why do you keep pulling away when we start to get close?"

He exhaled sharply as if frustration was doing him in. "I just need this to be over. I need to know you're safe."

"Billy Raquet is in jail."

"He's a suspect. We don't know that he's a killer or even the man who left you the threatening note. Until I'm sure, I have to keep all of my attention centered on protecting you."

She had no argument for that. "I'm really tired," she said. "And tomorrow will be really busy again, so I think I'll turn in."

He made no move to stop her as she trudged upstairs to spend another night alone in her lonesome bed. Nick had only been in her life a few days, but already she couldn't imagine life without him.

BY MIDAFTERNOON on Wednesday, frustration, fatigue and humidity had taken their toll on Jacinth's body. Worse, the thoughts that were kicking about in her mind today were giving her a serious headache.

She kicked disgustedly into a pile of dry leaves and

then plopped down on an old iron bench behind the carriage house.

"I've had it for today. If there's any sign of a secret passageway around here, it will take a stick of dynamite to uncover it."

Nick wiped his sleeve across the sweat that beaded his forehead. "You need a shower and a nap."

"I have another idea. Why don't we both shower and make a trip to the nursing home where my grandmother lived just before her death?"

Nick propped a foot on the side rung of the bench. "Any special reason?"

"I've had this sickening premonition all morning that Marie knew the killer well and was aware that he was killing women in her house."

"I got the impression that you were looking for the good in Marie."

"I was. She's my father's mother. She's my grandmother. I desperately need to find the good in her, but I can't ignore facts."

Two sons murdered, Jacinth thought.

One daughter-in-law who shut Marie entirely out of her life.

At least three young women murdered, mutilated and left to rot in the walls.

"I'm just looking for the truth," she said. "No matter how perverse it turns out to be."

THE NURSING HOME was nothing like Jacinth had anticipated. She'd expected dreary and institutional gray. Instead, the walls were a pale yellow. The carpet was stone-brown with dark yellow flecks that complemented the walls and off-white silk drapes.

A huge bouquet of purple and gold mums graced the dark mahogany table where they stopped to sign in.

A worker in a fitted pantsuit walked over to greet them. "Good afternoon. Welcome to Sunnydale. Are you to hear to see one of our guests?"

"No. This may sound like a strange request, but my grandmother was living here before she died last year. I never really knew her, but I was wondering if I could talk to someone who worked here during her stay."

"What was your grandmother's name?"

"Marie Villaré."

The woman's smiled brightened considerably. "You must be Caitlyn's sister. She came here with the same request a few months back."

"Yes, and she fell in love with a couple of your current guests."

"They fell in love with her, too."

"I'm Jacinth and this is Nick Bruno, a good friend of mine."

"It's nice to meet you both. And I'm Marilyn Shelby, the administrator at Sunnydale. Actually, I knew Marie as well as anyone around here. Why don't you two join me in my office and I'll be happy to try and answer your questions."

A very senior citizen with a slow gait and a twinkle in her eyes latched on to Jacinth's arm as they walked down the hall.

"Hello," Jacinth said. "How are you?"

The woman squeezed Jacinth's arm. "Let's get ice cream."

"You've had your ice cream," Marilyn said.

The woman chuckled as if she'd played a trick on them.

"That's Beth," Marilyn said. "She asks everyone for ice cream when they come in."

"At least she knows what she likes," Nick said.

Once in the office they settled around a small desk. "What is it you'd like to know about Marie?" Marilyn asked.

"Did she have many visitors?"

"Not many, but she wasn't lonesome. She made friends with the staff and the other guests. In fact, she engaged with them more than she did with her few visitors. I remember this one fairly regular caller that she'd totally ignore."

"Who was that?"

"The name Percy rings a bell, but I could be wrong. I think he was a friend of the family, but he might have been a relative."

Jacinth hadn't heard mention of a Percy in connection with Marie. "How often did he visit?"

"It wasn't daily or even weekly. I'd say more like every three weeks or so. If I remember correctly, he never stayed more than a few minutes."

"How long do you keep copies of your sign-in sheets?" Nick asked.

"They're on file at our corporate office indefinitely, but we only keep them here for three months."

"We'd like a copy of all of Marie's visitors during the time she lived here."

"I can get that for you, but it may take a few days."

"We need them by tomorrow." He took out a business card and handed it to her. "Please fax them to this number."

"I'll see what I can do."

"Do you remember any specifics about this particular visitor?"

Marilyn looked at Nick. "He was tall, about your height. Burlier. Big arms. Blond hair. I'd guess him to be in his late forties, but he might have been older."

That didn't sound like the description Detective Green had given of Billy Raquet.

"I don't think Marie appreciated his visits," Marilyn added.

"Why do you say that?" Nick asked.

Marilyn smiled. "She'd lie completely still, almost as if she were faking a coma. It was so exaggerated that the first time he came, one of the aides actually thought she'd had a stroke."

"But she hadn't?"

"No, but her performance is probably why I remember Percy as well as I do. The aides joked that he was so boring that Marie played dead rather than talking to him. They all peeked in her door whenever he stopped by."

"How was she after he left?"

"Just like normal. Watching TV, reading, visiting with her friends in the rec room. But she never talked about him. Whenever we'd ask her how Percy was, she'd get that blank look like she had no idea who we were talking about. Marie was a sly one."

"What's the chance you caught this man on camera?" Nick asked.

"Everyone who visits is caught on camera. But after six months, those records have to be requested by someone in law enforcement."

"That can be arranged," Jacinth said.

"If tracking this man down is important, you should look in Marie's black notebook. She wrote in it constantly. I'd think he'd merit at least a line or two."

This was definitely the first Jacinth had heard of a notebook. "Was she keeping a journal?"

"We had no clue what she was writing. She wouldn't let anyone read it. We teased her about having a movie made from her memoires."

"What happened to the notebook?"

"I'm sure it was returned to the family with her clothes and personal belongings. That's normally done right away."

"I was given the boxes from Sunnydale," Jacinth said, "but there was no notebook. Had there been, I'm sure I would remember."

"That's odd." Marilyn picked up a pencil and tapped the eraser end against her desk. "Let me check one place it might have disappeared to. I'll be right back."

Marilyn retuned less than five minutes later, a small thick black notebook in hand. She handed it to Jacinth.

"Where did you find it?"

"One of the ladies Marie spent a lot of time with had it in the drawer by her bed. When I asked her if she'd seen it, she said she was saving it for Marie. I'm really sorry about this."

"I'm just glad to have it now."

Jacinth opened the notebook and thumbed through the lined pages. The handwriting was mildly shaky but definitely legible. The margins were even. And it was even divided into sections.

Jacinth turned to the first page.

The Early Years.

I was six years old when I got my first hint that I was not a true Villaré. I was devastated.

This was exactly what Jacinth needed.

She prayed she wouldn't regret reading it.

Nathanial and I were blessed with a love for each other that few people ever know. I would have followed him to the ends of the earth.

Instead we chose the Villaré mansion on Esplanade Avenue where generations of Villarés had lived before us.

Their spirit gave me strength.

Their bravery gave me courage.

Their inspiration gave me guidance.

I cherish the wonderful blessings of the life Nathanial and I lived together, but if offered the chance to live it over again, I'd say no.

Our beloved son Micah brought us undreamed-of joy, far more than I deserved. But the pain of losing him at such an early age was almost too much to bear. I could never live through that kind of agony again.

Losing all contact with his daughters made his death even more heartbreaking. It was years before I forgave Sophie, but I finally realize that she was only trying to protect Jacinth and Caitlyn.

My greatest regret is that I failed my stepson. His was a sickness of the soul and mind. I should have insisted Nathanial get treatment for him. When I finally did make the decision to have him committed to a mental facility, he found out and ran away to Alaska. His blood is on my hands.

My life is now nearing the end. I go with God and joy that I will soon be reunited with Nathanial, Micah and all the Villarés that have gone before me.

I bequeath the house on Esplanade to my granddaughters in hopes that they find comfort and inspiration in understanding that the house has known joy and sorrow, laughter and tears, life and death.

But, above all, the Villaré Mansion on Esplanade Avenue in the heart of New Orleans, Louisiana, has known love.

Tears fell from Jacinth's eyes as she read the final pages of Marie's detailed journal. She and Nathanial had faced daunting challenges, yet their devotion to each other had remained strong until the end. Theirs was a true love story.

And in spite of what was recorded in the family Bible, they had not been brother and sister. Marie's mother, Elizabeth, had so desperately wanted a baby girl that when one of their young servants died in child-birth, leaving the infant an orphan, Elizabeth had taken the baby as her own.

But after reading her memoires, it seemed to Jacinth that Marie was more *Villaré* than any of her adopted brothers except perhaps for Nathanial.

The other brothers had moved away and willingly given up any claim to the Villaré property, the estate having dwindled to financial ruin by then.

There were many references to the sapphire brooch, but no mention of who should receive the valuable heir-loom. Perhaps Marie had intended to take the secret of its whereabouts with her to the grave.

Jacinth understood her grandmother much better now, but she still had questions that might never be answered.

Marie had written that Sophie fled with her two daughters after Micah's death in fear that whoever had killed Micah might harm them.

But if that were true, why hadn't Jacinth's mother returned after the killer had gone to prison? Why had she refused to ever speak of their father's family or of New Orleans?

Jacinth would love to share all she'd learned with Nick, but it was too late to bother him tonight. She should go to bed herself. Tomorrow would likely be another grinding day.

Perhaps she should ask Nick to take her fishing.

But getting close to Nick only to have him turn away from her was entirely too unsettling. So no matter that the attraction between them was breathtaking and mind-boggling...

No matter that his kisses drove her out of her mind...

No matter that he was so protective of her that he wouldn't leave her alone in this house for a second...

When the danger was past, she knew he would just walk away.

What would the brave Victoria Villaré have to say about that?

Victoria would have marched right down to Nick's room and demanded satisfaction, that's what.

So what was stopping Jacinth from doing the same?

Jacinth hesitated for less than a minute before she stepped out of her practical cotton pajamas with the cute little bunnies. The she went to the closet and wrapped her naked body in her luxurious silk robe.

Her insides quaked as she padded down the hallway to the next bedroom. She didn't even bother to knock, but just stepped inside—to an empty room and a bed that had not been slept in.

But Nick wouldn't have left the house without telling her. He was likely downstairs on the internet or watching TV. Still, the fight had been knocked out of her.

She started back to her room, but Sin was yowling about something near the head of the stairs. When Jacinth walked over to check on her, Sin quit yowling, ignored Jacinth and pranced away.

"What's with Sin?" Nick called from the foot of the stairs.

Jacinth's pulse quickened. She didn't respond to Nick's question, but she struck her sultriest pose—at least she hoped it was sultry—and paraded down the winding staircase.

Nick was still watching when she reached the landing. Jacinth gave one quick glance toward Victoria, who had been returned to her place of honor.

Then she dropped her robe, stepped over it and vamped her way to Nick.

Chapter Fifteen

Desire walloped Nick, knocking his feet practically out from under him as he watched Jacinth descend the wide staircase. All his pistons fired at once. His body quaked.

Don't do it, he told himself.

Don't do it.

Don't do it.

But then he opened his arms and Jacinth stepped inside them. The need he'd been fighting ever since he'd first laid eyes on her exploded inside him.

He kissed her over and over, ravaging her mouth, and still he couldn't get enough. Her salty, sweet taste intoxicated him. Her thrusting tongue and the mingling of their breaths set him on fire.

He splayed his hands across her back, reveling in the softness of her bare skin. He inched them lower, his fingers circling and kneading until he cupped her firm buttocks in his hands.

She arched toward him, and he lifted her only to release her so that she rode down the hard, throbbing length of his erection. Even through his jeans, the movement delivered excruciating stimulation.

He put his mouth to her ear, nibbling and sucking her lobe. "You are driving me absolutely mad, Jacinth."

"Don't stop, Nick. Please, don't stop."

"I don't think I can."

Tormented, he took her in his arms and started to carry her to her bed.

"Not upstairs, Nick. It's too far." She planted kisses on his neck, wantonly interspersing the sweet kisses with devouring sucks and nibbles.

He carried her into the den and laid her on the furry green rug near the hearth. The logs in the stone fireplace weren't lit, but the room was steamy warm.

Jacinth stretched out on her back, her knees bent, her triangle of dark hair in full, inviting view. Nick propped himself up on one elbow, his gaze soaking up every inch of her. She was beautiful, from the thick, silky locks that brushed her cheeks to her painted red toenails.

But he'd been with gorgeous women before. None had ever affected him like Jacinth did. It was all he could do to keep his hands off her if they just passed in the hall. He couldn't look at her mouth without wanting to taste her lips.

He'd physically ached to make love to her since the night they met.

But the need to protect her was even stronger. To protect her from a brutal killer. To protect her from himself.

What the hell was he doing now?

He rolled away.

Jacinth tugged him back. She took his hand and guided it to the swell of first one perfect breast and

194 Stranger, Seducer, Protector

then the other. Her nipples grew hard and erect beneath his thumb.

"Suck them, Nick. Please, suck them."

Desire ran roughshod over him. He cupped both her breasts and played with them each in turn. Tasting, nibbling, sucking as Jacinth moaned softly and writhed with pleasure.

Then she took his hand again. Holding it in both of hers, she guided it to the slick opening between her thighs. Her fingers tangled with his, both of them exploring and dipping into the heated wetness.

With the pressure bordering on agonizing, Nick extricated his hand from hers so that he could unzip his jeans. He managed to wiggle out of them and his shorts while Jacinth tugged the T-shirt over his head.

Once he was naked beside her, she cradled his erection in both hands, stroking its burgeoning length.

"Jacinth, if you—"

She kissed his words away and then touched her lips to the tip of his erection. Blood rushed to his head in dizzying waves.

"I need you inside me, Nick. I need you the way I've never needed any other man."

Reasons he shouldn't do this flooded his mind, but Jacinth's hands and mouth were doing all the wrong things in all the right ways.

He was going crazy with wanting her. He couldn't think. He didn't want to think. All he wanted was Jacinth.

He shifted on top of her and she wrapped her gorgeous legs around him. Desire roared through his veins as he thrust his full, throbbing length deep inside her and let the maddening hunger for her have its way.

JACINTH'S PULSE FINALLY stilled. Passion spent, she settled into the afterglow. She'd never been to such heights of exhilaration before. Had never allowed herself to let go of all her inhibitions and make love with every fiber of her being.

She couldn't have done it with anyone but Nick. He was everything she'd ever dreamed of in a man.

Tough. Indomitable. Exciting. Sexy. Romantic.

But he was also a protector, determined to keep her safe whether she appreciated his efforts or not. And even though she knew he wanted her, he'd been dogged about keeping her at arm's distance.

Thankfully, they'd passed that hurdle tonight.

She cuddled against him.

Nick rolled off the rug, then stood and pulled on his jeans. When he turned and faced her, he looked like a man standing in front of a firing squad.

"What's wrong?" she asked, her voice a low, shaky whisper.

"We have to talk."

Chapter Sixteen

Nick hated himself for what he'd done. He hated himself even more for what he had to do now. Making love with Jacinth had been even more perfect than he'd imagined in his wildest fantasies. And he'd had countless fantasies starring her over the past few days.

If a genie appeared at this minute and offered Nick three wishes, his choices would be easy. He'd wish for Jacinth to be in his bed, in his life and in his heart for the rest of his life.

But there were no genies. There were just the hard, punishing realities of life.

"I'm not who you think I am, Jacinth."

"You're married. I knew it."

He looked at her as if she'd lost her mind. "I'm not married. Just let me get through this, Jacinth."

"Please do, Nick—if that's your name."

"It's my name. I'm Nick Bruno, the only son of Elton Bruno. My father has spent the last twenty-one years in prison for the murder of Micah Villaré."

JACINTH'S CHEST CONSTRICTED. She couldn't breathe. She couldn't think. She couldn't move.

The shock slowly dissolved, replaced by blinding fury. "Get out of my house, Nick."

"Let me explain, Jacinth."

"I don't want to hear any more of your lies."

"My father didn't kill your father. He's innocent. I have to find a way to prove that."

She stood, grabbed a throw from the sofa and wrapped it around her naked body. Still, she'd never felt so exposed or so horribly defiled.

"You knew I lived here when you rented the Findleys' carriage house. You insinuated yourself into my life from that very first night. Even the kiss was part of your plan, wasn't it?"

"Falling for you was never part of the plan."

"What do you want from me, Nick? To plead for your father's parole while mine's bones lie at the bottom of a muddy bayou? That's it, isn't it?"

"I wanted the truth, Jacinth. That's all I've ever wanted."

"And how did you expect to get that from me?"

"All I know is that someone knows the truth and they didn't come forward. Your mother ran away even before your father's memorial service."

"She was afraid."

"Afraid of whom? Certainly not my father. He was arrested almost immediately. Yet Sophie never once returned to New Orleans. You said yourself she never even wanted to speak of it or of Micah's family."

Jacinth started to shake, the anger boiling inside her.

"You planned to use me to help pin Micah's murder on my mother. Now that she's dead, you'd besmirch her reputation and desecrate everything she's ever touched in her life, including Caitlyn and me.

"And I played right into your hands. Falling for you. Throwing myself at you. Forcing you to make love with me. And it was just part of your game."

"You know that's not true, Jacinth. There's no way you could believe that what we just shared wasn't real. I…" His words faltered.

"Get out, Nick."

"Don't be ridiculous, Jacinth. Things are too up in the air with the murders and heating up fast."

"The police have made an arrest."

"They've arrested a suspect. They have no proof that the real killer is not still out there. And if he is, he believes you have a three-quarter-million-dollar brooch that he's willing to kill for."

"I'll hire someone else to protect me."

"Fine. But until he shows, I'm on duty and I'm not leaving you alone."

"Because you think my getting killed will blow your scheme?"

"Because I don't think I'd want to keep living if I let that monster get to you."

Traitorous tears burned in her eyes, but she refused to fall for Nick's lies again. She grabbed the heavy brass lamp from the table, yanking the cord from the outlet as she did.

"Get out, or I swear I'll throw this at you."

"Be reasonable, Jacinth. You know I won't—"

She threw the lamp as hard as she could, not at Nick but at the marble fireplace.

The crash echoed through the house as Jacinth turned and ran up the stairs and into her room, slamming the door behind her. Her shattered heart stayed behind, the pieces nestled in the rug in her den.

NICK LET HIMSELF out the door and locked it behind him. He didn't want to chance Jacinth's coming out of her room later and finding him still in the house. It would upset her all over again.

He'd handled everything wrong. He'd known Jacinth would feel betrayed by his lies when she found out that he was Elton Bruno's son. And his asinine comments about her mother definitely hadn't helped his cause.

And all of it coming right after they'd made the most passionate love of his life. Now she even believed that was a lie. She hated him and probably had every reason to.

Not that it would have changed anything, but if he was going to tell her the truth, he should have told her the full truth.

He should have told her that he loved her.

Chapter Seventeen

Something hairy crept up his leg. Likely a spider that had crawled from beneath the dry, brown leaves at the foot of the tree. He squashed it between his jeans and his flesh without letting it break his concentration.

The front door to the decrepit Villaré mansion had just opened.

He watched as Nick Bruno stepped out and then locked the door behind him. Evidently, Jacinth's protector had decided she no longer needed his constant observation. After all, the man they believed had killed last fall's three luscious victims was in jail.

Nick cut across the lawn toward the Findley property. Jacinth Villaré was finally alone.

Tonight he'd finally revisit his lovely bones and add another skull to his collection. And while he was there, he'd retrieve the family heirloom that should have gone to him, the same way the Villaré house should be his.

He would give up the house. He would not give up the brooch. The money he'd get from it would buy him a new life somewhere far away from New Orleans. Maybe in Alaska.

Bodies decayed far more slowly in the cold.

Chapter Eighteen

Jacinth lay listless on the bed. Her body felt totally drained, but her tear-swollen eyes refused to close.

She had no one to blame for this but herself. Emboldened by Marie's diary and Victoria's inspiration, Jacinth had taken chances with her heart that she'd have never taken before.

She'd never make that mistake again.

Yet making love with Nick had been the most exciting, thrilling, heart-stopping moments of her life. How could she be sorry for that?

And how would she ever forget his smile, his cocky swagger, his touch, his kiss? How would she ever stop aching for Nick?

The anger dissolved into a pain so intense her heart felt as if it were being ripped from her chest. How could this possibly hurt so much?

Jacinth was startled by the most forlorn yowl she'd ever heard come from Sin. The yowl persisted, growing louder each time.

Jacinth put on her pajamas and jumped up to rescue the curious feline from whatever catastrophe she'd gotten herself into this time. She opened her bedroom door and looked down the dimly lit hallway. No Sin in sight.

But the musty odor was back, more overpowering than before.

Her bare feet padding on the polished wood, Jacinth followed Sin's cries to Marie's bedroom. Sin had somehow pushed the door shut again.

Jacinth turned the knob, flicked on the light and stepped into the bedroom. Sin was not alone.

"Finally, we meet."

Jacinth tried to run, but the man grabbed her by her hair and dragged her back into the bedroom. When she tried to break free again, he shoved her to the floor and put a heavy booted foot to her chest.

"That's no way to treat guests to the Villaré mansion."

Paralyzing fear swept through her. "Who are you?"

"Your long-lost half uncle. Your father must have spoken of me. Oh, that's right. Micah didn't live to talk. We were all so sad to see him go."

"You lie. You're not Luther. I've seen pictures of Luther and he looks nothing like you."

"You think I lie? You think I'm dead? I'll show you dead, Jacinth. And I'll let you meet it."

He moved his foot from her chest and when she struggled to a standing position, he shoved her against the wall and pressed his sweaty body against her. Her stomach lurched. The nauseating stench came from him.

She tried to push him off her, but he was too strong.

He pulled both arms behind her and twisted until she fell to her knees, crying in pain.

"What do you want?"

"Only what's rightfully mine."

"The house?"

He brandished a razor-sharp hunting knife that she hadn't seen coming and pressed the point of the blade to the back of her neck.

"I want the sapphire brooch. I want it now! And no tricks, Jacinth. I won't be fooled by the imitation."

The one thing she couldn't give him.

She had to think and think fast. "I'm not foolish enough to keep something that valuable at home, Luther. It's in a safe-deposit box. I can pick it up as soon as the bank opens tomorrow morning."

"Then give me the key."

"And then you'll kill me? I'm not stupid, Luther. If you want the key, you'll have to let me go free."

"No worry. I'll come for the brooch later. I have other urges that must be satisfied tonight."

"If you hurt me, Nick Bruno will kill you."

Luther threw back his head and roared with the maniacal laugh of a madman.

"I'm not afraid of Nick. I'm too smart for him. I'm too smart for all of them."

But he would be afraid if Nick were here. And Nick would be here if she hadn't sent him home. He'd have protected her with his life. She'd erupted in anger and sense of betrayal without even giving him a chance to explain.

"We're going to take a little walk, Jacinth. You won't

share your treasure with me, but I'll share mine with you." The tip of the blade pierced her flesh and warm drops of blood rolled down her neck.

She couldn't fight Luther's strength and his knife. Her only chance was to outsmart him. She'd have to play along until she could think of some way to escape.

"Where are your treasures, Luther?"

"Don't worry. I'll show you. And then I'll let you join my private club. You'll like it. Your father's a member. He fought like a tiger when I initiated him. But he didn't have the knife."

"You killed my father."

"Don't sound so shocked. He deserved it. Marie and Dad thought he was so much better than me, but the time it mattered most, I bettered him."

Luther chuckled as if he'd let her in on some grand joke. With the knife still at her throat, he led her to the empty closet and shoved her inside.

"You said we were going for a walk. We can't walk in the closet, Luther. Let's go outside."

He reached over her head. She couldn't see what he was doing, but she heard a low click and then a soft whir as if he'd turned on a fan.

The back wall of the closet parted like a sliding door, leaving an opening no more than a foot wide.

"Victoria's secret passageway," she said, finally understanding how Luther had gotten into her house without setting off the alarm.

"But improved and modified throughout the years. My naive stepmother believed I'd had it sealed as she'd asked. She never once suspected that I'd merely improved it and hidden it from her."

A scream gurgled in her throat as Luther shoved her through the opening, but the second she opened her mouth, he slid the point of the blade to her jugular.

"Scream and you die."

And then the real nightmare began.

She stumbled along in the dark, the knife still at her throat. Something brittle crunched beneath her feet. And the stench grew so strong she became nauseated.

New fear pummeled her control. If she threw up the knife might slip and slice her jugular. The aged passageway grew so narrow in some places that Luther could barely squeeze through, but still, he pushed her on.

Her feet were bare, and she tripped over something that felt like a skull, or at least she imagined it to be.

Death lived within these walls and with every step she expected fleshless hands to grab her and pull her into her grave. Her skin grew clammy. Her heart felt as if it was about to explode out of her chest.

Just bones, she told herself. They couldn't hurt her. But Luther could. She had to regain control. If she didn't find a way to escape, she'd die in this hellhole of Luther's making.

Luther's voice grew excited as he told her about the passageway and how it tunneled under the ground for several yards before exiting through the floor of the rotting carriage house. Through a secret door so well disguised that she and Nick had not found it.

The narrow space tilted seriously to the left as they

squeezed around a corner. Luther turned on a flashlight and shot a beam of light in front of them. Her blood ran cold at the sight. Not one, but several mummified bodies in varying states of decay. And bones scattered about like pickup sticks.

They were not fakes.

"How many, Luther?" Her voice trembled. "How many people have you killed?"

"Fifteen women and Micah. He was the first, the most satisfying in many ways. Unfortunately, I couldn't stay around to watch his dead body being devoured by the hungry gators."

"Why? Why kill him? What had he ever done to deserve that?"

"Because he took everything I ever wanted. Even Sophie. I loved her first. Micah had to have her, just because she was mine. But no one hated him for stealing her from me. Dad and Marie just loved him all the more for giving them grandchildren."

No wonder her mother had taken Jacinth and Caitlyn and run away. She must have realized that Luther was a psychopath and been afraid of what he might do to her baby girls.

The knife pressed deeper into Jacinth's flesh and the hot trickle of blood began to flow again.

"I followed Micah to the old fishing cabin down the bayou that belonged to Elton's father," Luther said, his voice low and tinged with pleasure, as if he relished reliving the murder.

"Micah and Elton had fished and drunk the afternoon away. I waited until after dark and then when Micah walked down to the dock alone to check his traps, I slit his throat."

"And dropped his body into the bayou."

"I had to. If I'd gotten his blood in my car, I was the one who'd have gone to prison."

"Instead you let Elton Bruno go to jail for the crime."

"I did more than let him. I made sure he went to prison instead of me. His fingerprints were all over the fillet knife I stole from the camp house, along with Micah's blood. Once the cops found that in the palmettos behind the cabin, Elton went straight to the top of the suspect list."

"Why kill the others? Why kill innocent victims?"

"Innocent? You know nothing of innocent? They were users, just like your mother. She led me on, and then when I killed Micah and went to her, she cringed at my touch. I should have killed her that night. I almost did."

Luther was truly insane, but crazy like the proverbial fox. He'd gotten away with murder for years, killing women and entombing their bodies in this dark, dank crypt mere yards from where Marie slept. There must have been method to that madness, as well.

He'd even gotten away with faking his own murder to keep from being committed to a mental facility.

He'd come back to New Orleans when his stepmother was dying, but he'd only come back for the brooch and the money he could get for it.

"Our tour is over, Jacinth. I have to leave, but you don't have to go. You can stay with these lovely bones forever. But first, you will satisfy me the way your mother never did."

He pulled her close, her back to his chest. He took the blade from her throat and sliced through the top of her cotton pajamas.

No. She couldn't die. She couldn't leave Nick thinking she hated him. She wanted to live and go fishing with Nick. She wanted to dance with him in the moonlight. She wanted to tell him his father really was innocent and so was her mother. She wanted to spend her life loving Nick.

Only how could she live when with one flick of the knife at her throat she'd become just another of Luther's lifeless treasures.

Luther laughed as he cut the rest of the pajama top away. She kicked at him and tried to run, but he grabbed her and shoved her to the body-strewn floor.

There was no way out. She opened her mouth and screamed.

Chapter Nineteen

Stakeouts were nothing new to Nick. But he wasn't used to sitting around waiting on a madman to attack the woman he loved. Sitting in his truck trying to watch the house and listening and watching for any indication of danger just wasn't cutting it.

Jacinth was pissed as hell at him and she had every reason to be. But she couldn't be any madder if he was inside the house and at least then he'd be alerted at the first sign she was in any kind of jeopardy.

He raised the windows in his truck then slid out and locked the door behind him.

The scream came just as he fit the key in the lock of her front door. Panic hit hard and fast. He pulled his gun and raced up the stairs and to her bedroom. The bedside lamp was on. Her bed was empty.

"Jacinth!"

No answer. No screams. If he'd screwed this up and let something happen to her… No. He couldn't go there.

A light was on in one of the bedrooms. He checked it out, his finger poised on the trigger. The room smelled like rotting earth. A few specks of red dotted the carpet leading to the closet.

Fighting to stay in control, he rushed across the room, almost tripping over Sin. He righted himself and stared into a gaping hole in the back of the closet, like a giant mouth waiting for its food to be shoved inside.

Nick yanked his high-intensity LED penlight from his pocket and pushed through the opening and into a dank and narrow corridor. Bones and skulls peppered the floor. He'd stepped into a freakin' morgue inside the walls of Jacinth's house.

He fought a rush of near paralyzing fear that he might be too late. He had to keep focused, and he couldn't do that if he plummeted into anguish.

He slowed as he saw a spray of light up ahead, bouncing off the wall from around an angled corner. Someone was there and they would have heard him coming.

"Take one more step, Nick, and I'll slice her jugular. You know I will."

Nick froze. He'd know that voice anywhere.

Keeping his back against the wall and his Glock on ready, Nick eased around the corner.

His heart almost stopped when he spotted Jacinth slumped against Luther, her pajama top slashed, a knife at her throat.

She raised her gaze to meet his. "Luther killed Micah, Nick. Sliced his throat when—"

"Shut up, you bitch."

"That right, Luther? Did you let my father go to prison for your crime? You can tell the truth. You're not leaving here alive."

Nick's finger ached to pull the trigger now, but he couldn't risk it as long as Luther was holding the knife at Jacinth's jugular.

Nick stared at Luther. The man had a different face. The plastic surgeon had done a good job of changing his appearance. He was about the same age as Nick's father, but probably looked a good ten years younger. But then he hadn't spent half his life in prison.

"Still the coward, aren't you, Luther? Tough with the women. A wimp with the men."

"Shut up."

"Dad told me about you. Picked on some girl at school and her daddy came after you with a billy club. You were crying like a baby."

"I said shut up."

"Make me. Fight me with that knife, not Jacinth. Play fair and be a man for once in your life."

"I am a man."

"You won't walk out of here alive this way. You kill Jacinth, I kill you. Fight me fair and square and at least you have a chance. You've killed enough women. Let this one go."

Luther hesitated a second too long. Something moved behind Nick. And then Sin rounded the corner.

Startled, Luther jumped back. The knife left Jacinth's throat, giving Nick the shot he'd been waiting on. Nick pulled the trigger shooting Luther in the chest.

Luther kept coming, like some superhuman species. He slashed at Jacinth, missing her stomach by inches. The space was too narrow to dodge a swinging, stabbing knife.

Nick pulled the trigger again, hitting Luther right between the eyes. This time there was no doubt that Luther was down for the count.

Decades of evil had finally come to an end.

Nick reached for Jacinth's hand. "Are you okay?"

"I'm alive. Thanks to you."

"I told you I'd protect you." He led her out of the maze and then pulled her into his arms. "I'm sorry, Jacinth. I did everything wrong, but when I thought that monster might have killed you..." His voice broke. "I love you, Jacinth. I don't expect you to love me back, but I love you all the same."

"But I do love you back, Nick. I never thought love could come in a matter of days, not to me. But it came in a heartbeat. I love you. I love you so very much."

He kissed her and this time nothing in his life had ever felt so right.

Right now they had to invite Detective Greene to the party, but that was okay. There was no rush on sorting out the details. He planned to love Jacinth for the rest of his life.

Epilogue

Jacinth stood in front of the mirror in her bedroom, adjusting her veil for the hundredth time.

Caitlyn waltzed in balancing two flutes of champagne. She set them down next to an unopened legal-size packing envelope.

"Stop worrying. You look beautiful, and that brooch looks fantastic with the dress."

"Even if it's the copy."

"Who cares? It's gorgeous. Aren't you going to drink your champagne?"

"I couldn't possibly."

"I'm pretty sure there's no law against having a drink on your wedding day."

"My stomach is too unsettled. If I drink that I'll probably throw up in the middle of the ceremony."

"Drink it. It will make it easier on all of us."

"Are you sure Nick is here?"

"He's here. And so is my gorgeous husband, the best man. And so is the preacher. And so are dozens of your friends from the university and from Ohio."

"What about Nick's father?"

"Yes. He's here and looking good now that his cancer is in remission. Give it up, sis. Nothing bad is going to happen to ruin your big day. This is going to be a rocking wedding and reception."

"Something always happens around this house. I'll probably have a body fall out of the chandelier right when I start to say *I do*."

"Nope. No bodies in the walls. Passageway totally cleaned out and sealed. You're good to go." Caitlyn picked up the envelope. "What's this?"

"It was delivered by courier this morning."

Caitlyn ripped the envelope open.

Jacinth gasped. "Don't open that!"

"Why not? It's addressed to both of us."

"It's from Marie's attorney, probably informing us that we owe more back taxes. And I want this to be the most perfect day of my life."

"It will be perfect because you're marrying the man you love." Caitlyn reached into the envelope. "There's a box, no two boxes, and a letter. Which do I open first?"

"If you must open anything, go with the letter."

"Cool. The letter's from our grandmother." She read for a moment, then gasped. "Oh my God."

"What is it?"

"Grandma Marie was a manipulative little devil. Basically she says that if we stay in the house for one full year, we get the real-deal sapphire brooch. And one copy—which is all she had left. But then we already have the one you're wearing."

Caitlyn tore into the blue box. "Yeow! Now that's what I call jewelry. With this kind of sparkle, you may have to pass out sunglasses. Pin it on and take it for a test drive."

"Do we really want a three-quarter-of-a-million-dollar brooch when the house still needs so many repairs and we need to add another kitchen so that we can both have our separate living quarters?"

They both shook their heads at once.

"But you must wear it today," Caitlyn said, already pinning it on her in place of the copy. "It will be the perfect finishing touch for the perfect Villaré wedding."

The music started. "That's my cue as maid of honor. You're up next," she said, pulling Jacinth into a hug. "Happy Wedding Day."

When the wedding march started, Jacinth stopped at the head of the staircase, the fluttering in her stomach growing wilder by the second.

And then her gaze locked with Nick's and she forgot everything but him and how exciting it would be to share his life.

In the end, no matter what your name or how many sapphires and heirlooms you owned, it all came down to love.

* * * * *

INTRIGUE

COMING NEXT MONTH

Available November 8, 2011

#1311 CAMOUFLAGE COWBOY
Daddy Corps
Jan Hambright

#1312 SECRET PROTECTOR
Situation: Christmas
Ann Voss Peterson

#1313 DECODED
Colby Agency: Secrets
Debra Webb

#1314 GRAYSON
The Lawmen of Silver Creek Ranch
Delores Fossen

#1315 WESTIN FAMILY TIES
Open Sky Ranch
Alice Sharpe

#1316 WINTER HAWK'S LEGEND
Copper Canyon
Aimée Thurlo

You can find more information on upcoming
Harlequin® titles, free excerpts and more at
www.HarlequinInsideRomance.com.

Harlequin® Special Edition® is thrilled to present a new installment in USA TODAY *bestselling author RaeAnne Thayne's reader-favorite miniseries,* THE COWBOYS OF COLD CREEK.

Join the excitement as we meet the Bowmans—four siblings who lost their parents but keep family ties alive in Pine Gulch. First up is Trace. Only two things get under this rugged lawman's skin: beautiful women and secrets. And in Rebecca Parsons, he finds both!

Read on for a sneak peek of CHRISTMAS IN COLD CREEK. *Available November 2011 from Harlequin® Special Edition®.*

On impulse, he unfolded himself from the bar stool. "Need a hand?"

"Thank you! I…" She lifted her gaze from the floor to his jeans and then raised her eyes. When she identified him her hazel eyes turned from grateful to unfriendly and cold, as if he'd somehow thrown the broken glasses at her head.

He also thought he saw a glimmer of panic in those interesting depths, which instantly stirred his curiosity like cream swirling through coffee.

"I've got it, Officer. Thank you." Her voice was several degrees colder than the whirl of sleet outside the windows.

Despite her protests, he knelt down beside her and began to pick up shards of broken glass. "No problem. Those trays can be slippery."

This close, he picked up the scent of her, something fresh and flowery that made him think of a mountain meadow on a July afternoon. She had a soft, lush mouth and for one brief, insane moment, he wanted to push aside that stray lock of hair slipping from her ponytail and taste her. Apparently he needed to spend a lot less time working and a great deal *more* time recreating with the opposite sex if he could have sudden random fantasies about a woman he wasn't even inclined to like, pretty or not.

"I'm Trace Bowman. You must be new in town."

She didn't answer immediately and he could almost see the wheels turning in her head. Why the hesitancy? And why that little hint of unease he could see clouding the edge of her gaze? His presence was obviously making her uncomfortable and Trace couldn't help wondering why.

"Yes. We've been here a few weeks."

"Well, I'm just up the road about four lots, in the white house with the cedar shake roof, if you or your daughter need anything." He smiled at her as he picked up the last shard of glass and set it on her tray.

Definitely a story there, he thought as she hurried away. He just might need to dig a little into her background to find out why someone with fine clothes and nice jewelry, and who so obviously didn't have experience as a waitress, would be here slinging hash at The Gulch. Was she running away from someone? A bad marriage?

So…Rebecca Parsons. Not Becky. An intriguing woman. It had been a long time since one of those had crossed his path here in Pine Gulch.

Trace won't rest until he finds out Rebecca's secret, but will he still have that same attraction to her once he does? Find out in CHRISTMAS IN COLD CREEK. Available November 2011 from Harlequin® Special Edition®.

Harlequin®

ROMANTIC
SUSPENSE

CARLA CASSIDY

Cowboy's Triplet Trouble

Jake Johnson, the eldest of his triplet brothers, is stunned
when Grace Sinclair turns up on his family's ranch declaring
Jake's younger and irresponsible brother as the father of her
triplets. When Grace's life is threatened, Jake finds himself
fighting a powerful attraction and a need to protect. But as
the threats hit closer to home, Jake begins to wonder
if someone on the ranch is out to kill Grace....

A brand-new Top Secret Deliveries story!

TOP SECRET
DELIVERIES

Available in November wherever books are sold!

www.Harlequin.com

HRS27751

Harlequin®
Desire

ALWAYS POWERFUL, PASSIONATE AND PROVOCATIVE.

**NEW YORK TIMES AND USA TODAY
BESTSELLING AUTHOR**

BRENDA JACKSON

**PRESENTS A BRAND-NEW TALE
OF SEDUCTION**

TEMPTATION

TEXAS CATTLEMAN'S CLUB: THE SHOWDOWN

Millionaire security expert and rancher Zeke Travers
always separates emotion from work. Until a case
leads him to Sheila Hopkins—and the immediate,
scorching heat that leaped between them. Suddenly,
Zeke is tempted to break the rules. And it's only a
matter of time before he gives in....

Available November wherever books are sold.

www.Harlequin.com

HD73133